THE DOOR

A Door That Opens to a Dark, Suspenseful Spiritual World

THE DOOR

A Door That Opens to a Dark, Suspenseful Spiritual World

RICHARD J. KERR • STANFORD ERICKSON

A POST HILL PRESS BOOK
ISBN: 978-1-63758-348-7
ISBN (eBook): 978-1-63758-349-4

The Door:
A Door That Opens to a Dark, Suspenseful Spiritual World
© 2022 by Richard J. Kerr and Stanford Erickson
All Rights Reserved
Art by Andre Kerr

This novel is entirely a work of fiction. The names, characters, and incidents portrayed in it are the work of the authors' imagination. There is a reference to a historical character who started the town of Cassadaga. But any other reference to actual persons, living or dead, is entirely coincidental.

No part of this book may be reproduced, stored in a retrieval system, or transmitted by any means without the written permission of the author and publisher.

Post Hill Press
New York • Nashville
posthillpress.com

Published in the United States of America

1 2 3 4 5 6 7 8 9 10

Andre Kerr provided the drawings in this book. He is the son of Richard and a professional artist who showed his talent when still in a high chair. He has been involved in art and art projects his entire life. Currently in his sixties, he builds sets for TV and movies.

The thoroughness and dedication of Richard J. Kerr in conceiving the theme of the book and his drive in forcing me to contribute to it demonstrates to my mind why he was so successful and useful to our county in his 32 years with the CIA.

This is the first novel by Richard J. Kerr.
He published a book of short stories, *The Dark Side of Paradise*, in 2019 and a memoir of his life before, during, and after his time in the CIA titled *Unclassified* in 2020. The novel is based on one of his short stories enriched by contributions by Stanford Erickson.

CONTENTS

CHAPTER ONE

AN ACCIDENT OR SOMETHING ELSE

Elsie McKenzie was sitting at her desk staring at her computer screen. She was not working on the draft of her current book. She was woolgathering, or more precisely, thinking about several incidents that had happened over the past weeks.

All of these "incidents" involved her current unfinished book. Several times as she was pulling her evidence together, it seemed as if someone took over the computer or at least overrode what she was trying to record. The words that came out changed the facts or the point she was trying to make, and the criticisms she expressed were softened.

Even more worrisome, some new text appeared one morning that included ideas and thoughts she found objectionable and not at all in keeping with what she intended. Something or someone had changed her text without her permission. It was very irritating, and she was determined to find out exactly what was happening.

Elsie had published over a dozen whodunit novels. Now she was writing an exposé. But she seemed to be losing control of her text. She would write during the day, then send a copy to her editor and agent only to find that changes had been made overnight on the copy received by her editor and agent and on her computer as well. She had talked with her agent and told her what was happening. The agent, who only received the changed copy, seemed a bit skeptical that any changes were being made and suggested that maybe Elsie had forgotten what she had written. Elsie knew that was not the case. Her memory was perfectly good. She was certain she'd find the answer to why changes were being made to her text.

Trying to make sense out of the "mischief" that seemed to be shadowing her current writing caused her to think back to stories her Scottish grandfather had told about the fairies and trolls that had messed with people's lives. Had one of those creatures entered her writing life? She chuckled at the thought. Maybe they could come up with some interesting text that she could use, something she couldn't think up herself.

Music was always in the background when she wrote. Classic, jazz, and country music played on the radio without commercial interruptions. Her taste in music came from her father, at least the interest in classical and jazz. Country music was something she latched on to after going to a bluegrass festival with her now-deceased husband, Albert. Many of her friends kidded her about liking those "redneck" tunes, but she was a steadfast fan. It also helped remind her of the twenty-four years she shared with Albert. Thoughts about music also brought back those great memories of her husband. He had died at a young age, before she moved to Vero Beach where she now lived. She missed him terribly even though he had been gone for many years. They had a great marriage with many happy times. To this day, she still longed for the easy conversations over breakfast and dinner, the joking and teasing that made life so enjoyable. They had travelled a fair amount and particularly enjoyed cruising.

Because they were unable to have children, the focus of attention was on each other. She regretted not having children particularly as she grew older and had no one to talk with about their common past. Fortunately, as a teacher, she had watched hundreds of students grow up and had kept in touch with some of them. Still, children would have helped fill the void of losing Albert and living alone. She said to herself, "Stop feeling sorry for yourself. You have a pleasant life and some good friends, and you are a successful author." Those memories caused her to think about her nephew, Robert. She had a hand in raising him after his mother died, and she was very fond of him. In fact, he was kind of a substitute child. She had suffered through the trials of his being a teenager, and she had watched as he grew up. He had been a working detective in the Denver area for a number of years before moving to Vero Beach. Always on the lookout for information on criminal behavior and police techniques, Elsie had cast him as a character in some of her books and also found opportunities to weave in some of his stories about working as a detective as well. It helped her write stories that had a touch of realism to them. Like Robert, she found criminal behavior often repulsive but never boring.

Elsie wondered how much more she should tell Robert about her current book and her longtime interest in the supernatural. She had mentioned attending séances and trying to communicate with her dead husband. She wondered what Robert thought when she had mentioned some of this during dinner with him. She did not think he was particularly happy with her involvement in these "practices." But she had to live her life the way she thought best.

Listening for a moment to a song that seemed to fit with her current mood about not being promised a garden of roses, Elsie decided that what she needed was a cup of hot tea. Both her friend Sheila, who really was more like a companion, and her nephew, Robert, had tried to persuade her to bring a kettle upstairs to her office to avoid going up and down the stairs. She said the exercise did her good and that she needed breaks from writing.

She walked down the hall from her office and stood at the top of the stairs thinking about how she was going to get control of her writing. On the way down the hall, she thought she heard some noise coming from the bedroom next to her office—perhaps a door opening. She was reluctant to look into the bedroom because she was always a bit apprehensive about going into that particular room. It was the "door" inside the bedroom that bothered her. It had been placed at the end of the room and opened out to nothing—no stairs or balcony. Nothing! She knew that the door had been installed when the house was first built to allow spirits to come and go as they pleased. Elsie had never had the experience of seeing visiting spirits. Thank God! What would she have done if a spirit came tramping through the house? Probably faint dead away, although she was not the fainting type.

As she stood at the top of the stairs, she sensed some movement and heard a slight noise behind her. She started to turn, but before she could move, she felt hands pressing on her back, pushing her forward.

She hurtled down the stairs.

CHAPTER TWO

THE POLICE GET INVOLVED

Sheila had driven over from her condo on the island. She loved the drive along Route 101 and often turned onto the street that ran past the Ocean Grill and ended at the beach. She would stop at the end of the circular road and look out over the ocean. It was beautiful, with small waves generated by a southwest wind breaking on the white sand. This time of year, there were only a few people on the beach—too early for sunbathers, so only some hardy swimmers. There was no traffic, so she could sit in her car for a few minutes watching the ocean and admiring the puffy white clouds that slowly moved across the sky. She never tired of this view. It was calming and peaceful.

Driving across the bridge to the town of Vero Beach was less peaceful, although traffic this time of year was manageable. The northerners had arrived in Vero Beach after Thanksgiving or just before Christmas, and those pushy drivers from the north, particularly those from New York and New Jersey, disturbed the quiet little city of Vero Beach. The population of the town more than doubled during the winter, and restaurants became crowded. It was no longer possible to walk down the center of the street on the island. Nevertheless, the town was still the jewel of Florida.

Sheila stopped at the store and picked up something for the two of them to eat with their coffee. Sheila was on her way for her twice-weekly gab session with Elsie McKenzie. Her weekly routine also involved stopping at Panera Bread and picking up three scones. One for each of them, and one to share. Sheila liked the raspberry scones, Elsie the orange-flavored scones, and they shared the blueberry scone.

Sheila parked the car in front of the two-story house in the old part of Vero Beach. Her friend Elsie had bought the house over twenty years ago, soon after she retired from teaching school in Virginia and shortly after her husband, Albert, died. The two had met at a Vero Beach book club and become close friends. Sheila visited several times a week bringing breakfast, lunch, or snacks. They talked about their time as teachers as they drank coffee and ate their tasty sweets. Sheila had been a librarian so the two had a lot in common.

Sheila walked her usual route around the back of the house, looking at the flowerbeds and lawn to see if the gardeners were keeping up. She thought she would tell them to cut back some of the Brazilian pepper and put down some mulch on the beds. She took it upon herself to make sure the yard was in order. Elsie did not pay much attention to the outside.

Before she went into the house, Sheila looked up at the door on the second floor. It opened out onto nothing. It had no earthly function. That was the problem, wasn't it? No *earthly* function. So why was it there? Elsie had explained that the first owner of the house believed in spirits, and this door allowed them access.

Sheila thought this was all spiritual mumbo jumbo. She thought to herself that if she had been asked, her advice would have been not to buy a house with such a strange history. Who knows whether it was haunted or had some gruesome history? Elsie did not find living in the house alone to be frightening, even at night. Her office was upstairs, just down the hall from the room with the door. The whole thing sent a chill down Sheila's spine. Thank goodness she did not live here and only visited during daylight hours.

She unlocked the back door with the key she kept on the ring that held her car keys, opened the door, and walked into the kitchen. She was surprised that the lights in the kitchen were not on. Usually by this time in the morning Elsie had coffee on and was eating breakfast. Perhaps she had gotten busy working on her book. She placed the scones purchased that morning at "yuppie" Panera on the kitchen counter and went looking for the lady of the house.

Walking into the hall, she realized after a moment that there was an object at the bottom of the stairs. Letting out a gasp, she quickly realized it was Elsie's body. Sheila moved quickly, quicker than she had moved in a few years, and felt for a pulse, finding none. Elsie was cold—and clearly dead. Catching her breath, she thought she might call Elsie's doctor but realized that it was too late for medical help and instead dialed 911.

"I found my dear friend dead at the bottom of her stairs. I regularly visit her at home. I think she's dead. It's such a shock. I checked her pulse. No pulse. Please send someone, please?"

Sheila gave the address and feeling a bit faint, went into the kitchen to sit and wait for the police. Minutes later, a police car pulled up next to her car and two officers got out. Sheila unlocked the front door and opened it to let the officers in.

The older of the two officers spoke first, asking, "Did you make the call about finding someone dead?"

She recounted coming into the house and finding Elsie McKenzie at the bottom of the stairs. The officer asked her to show them. She took them into the hall where Elsie's body lay. The older officer felt for a pulse.

"She seems awfully cold. She probably fell last night." He asked Sheila, "Is there another set of stairs?"

Sheila said, "There is another stairway to the second floor in the kitchen."

The older officer went into the kitchen to find the stairs and go up to the top of the floor. The younger officer who appeared to be more senior stayed behind to ask Sheila some questions.

"How did you get into the house?"

"I regularly visit during the week. I am sort of a companion to Elsie, so she gave me a key."

"Are you the only person other than the owner to have a key?"

Sheila thought for a moment, and then said, "A nephew, who lives on the island, may have a key. He often visits Elsie. You probably can find his number—Robert McKenzie—in the Rolodex in her office." Sheila had gotten to know Robert rather well. He regularly visited Elsie and sometimes asked Sheila to join him and Elsie for dinner. He was a very good conversationalist and rather charming.

The officer came down from upstairs, and the two officers took a quick look around the house, checking doors and windows. They called for a police medical examiner and asked Sheila when she had last seen or talked with Elsie McKenzie. Sheila explained that Elsie and she habitually met a few times each week. The last time she was with Elsie was two days ago. The older officer asked if Elsie had any problems with walking up or down stairs.

"Elsie was in excellent health, for her age," she said. "She tended to walk on the beach at least twice a week for a mile or so."

Looking at the bag clutched in Sheila's hand, the older officer asked what was in it.

"Scones for Elsie and me."

Sheila looked at each officer and knew she needed to then say, "There's one for each of us if you like."

* * *

Later, as they left the house, the younger officer thought the dead woman resembled his grandmother. He had been called to houses where there had been serious falls several times in his career. He guessed that many of the people who fell ended up in rehab centers and some never recovered. Maybe he should check his grandmother's house and see if railings were needed. She lived in a one-story house, but there were steps here and there. He wrote a note to himself on a notepad.

The two officers left the house but stood next to their car talking. "When I went upstairs, I opened the doors to the office and the bedroom. In the bedroom there's a door that opens out into the air. Come around to the back, and I'll show you." The two of them walked around to the back of the house, and the older officer pointed up at the door that opened into midair. "That is really strange, but I don't see any connection between it and the death of the old lady."

A short time later, the medical examiner arrived. After examining the body, he decided an autopsy was necessary. The doctor then called to have the body removed. The police and the doctor agreed that the death appeared to be an accident, but an autopsy would show if drugs or alcohol were involved.

CHAPTER THREE

MY POOR AUNT

I got involved in this drama when the police called informing me my aunt had died in an accident. Poor Aunt Elsie; she was a dear, and I felt real loss and regret. The two of us were the last of the immediate McKenzie family. We had been quite close and often got together for dinner or just to visit. She was twenty-five years my senior, but the age difference did not seem to matter. I enjoyed her company. She had also helped raise me after my mother died unexpectedly when I was in my teens.

Just the week before, the two of us had gone out to dinner at the signature restaurant in Vero Beach—the Ocean Grill—and had a delightful time. I remembered with pleasure that we both had a couple of dirty gin martinis and scrumptious dinners. She liked the Grill's seafood, and I liked the steaks. I also recalled that she was worried about her current book. I am interested in writing and recently published a book of short stories—so we had that in common, although she was a recognized author with a long string of published successes.

Nevertheless, she often confided to me about problems with a plot or with writer's block.

During our last dinner together, she had said her current problems were a bit different than any she'd encountered before. Her writing seemed to be changing on its own and moving in directions that she did not like. She said she was writing an exposé of a church and spiritualist group. When she became too critical, she said, her derogatory words were either edited out or the criticism was muted a bit.

I was a bit puzzled. After all, she controlled the word processor. Elsie did not have a good explanation beyond saying that she had talked to authors who had felt their scripts were moving ahead without their consciously thinking about them. It was as if the story assumed a life of its own. I thought at the time I understood what she was saying. Even in my limited experience as a writer I had times when the story took on its own pace and events seemed to develop without my intervention.

I asked her what she was "exposing" in her current book. She laughed and said, "Some years ago I began consulting spiritualists trying to get in touch with my dead husband, Albert. That is when I first heard about the Spiritual and Health Camp located north of Vero Beach. I visited the camp and tried to contact Albert using several different mediums. I had modest success and made it a regular practice to visit the camp a couple of times each year. I became a patron, giving some money to support the facility and even serving for a short period on its board of trustees. Then the camp got a new minister and director, and things began to change.

"The new leader—a beautiful, aggressive woman—began a major publicity effort trying to raise attendance at the camp. She brought in some famous spiritualists to give lectures and pushed the various mediums to encourage contributions and long-term gifts to the camp. The camp was turned into a business and lost some of its charms and innocence. Most important and most worrisome was that the new minister and director of the camp, Abigale Cruz, seemed to be changing its character. Rather than a community, she was trying to develop a cult following. Everything was built around her forecasts and predictions, her communication with those on the other side, and her direct communication with the spirits. I did not like the changes and believed that people were being exploited. That's when I began a serious investigation of what was going on at the camp. A lot of money was coming in, and I wondered what was being done with it. I started writing the new book."

My aunt was a pretty determined character, and I did not envy those who were about to receive the full force of her criticism. Kidding her, I did say, "Be careful when you take on the spirits or the dark world. Who knows how they might retaliate." The look my aunt gave me, now that I recall, was startling to me. I thought I saw fear, absolute fear, in her expression. Those words, by me, would haunt me.

CHAPTER FOUR

SUSPICIONS TAKE ROOT

I still have the curiosity of a detective, and I was a bit puzzled by my aunt's "accident." I went into medical retirement after a serious auto accident, but I was a detective with the Denver Police Department for a number of years. I had a lot of spare time now and thought I would look into the details of her fall.

The next day, I called the police and asked to speak to one of the officers that had come to the house. Officer Ben Conners, the officer in charge of the case, rang back a short time later. I told him I wanted to talk to someone who had been at the scene of my aunt's accident.

"Was there anything unusual on the stairs or about her fall? Were all the doors and windows locked, and was there any sign that someone had been in the house when she fell?"

Conners responded rather quickly, saying, "There was no evidence to suggest this was anything other than an accident." He added, "It's not unusual, in my experience, that elderly people are injured in a fall. In this case it occurred at the top of stairs and was fatal."

He then paused and seemed to be thinking.

"I was struck by how far down the stairs she first hit. Like she had gone headfirst. You could see where her head struck the stairs because her glasses put a dent in the wood, and the lens was broken at that time."

I thanked the officer for calling back, sat back, and thought about what to do next. I decided I would call the medical examiner in the next day or two and ask about the autopsy. When I got around to calling the office of the medical examiner, I was told that to get a copy of the autopsy I needed to fill out a request form. I said, "I'm not interested in the details of the autopsy, but as next of kin I would like to talk with the doctor who conducted it."

The secretary said she would have the doctor call me. A few hours later, Doctor Theodore Agee called and told me he had done the autopsy on my aunt.

"Was there anything out of the ordinary in this particular accident?"

The doctor was silent for a moment and then answered, "There was a significant amount of trauma to the head, neck, and shoulders, more than I have ever seen for an accident involving a senior falling down stairs. There was no indication that alcohol or drugs were involved. The injuries suggest she fell down the steps headfirst."

I asked, "What kind of shoes was she wearing?"

He again paused for a moment before answering. "I believe she was wearing tennis or walking shoes, definitely not heels or dress shoes."

I thanked him for the information and put down the phone, feeling a bit more confused than when I had begun the conversation. I had a vague feeling that the accident was not as simple as it first seemed. Was I making a mountain out of a molehill? Maybe, but it would not hurt to look into what my aunt was up to and what she might have discovered about the camp.

CHAPTER FIVE

THE INVESTIGATION BEGINS

I decided to go to my aunt's house and look for a will and any instructions on how she wished to be treated after her death. The house had a musky foul smell to it. I found the thermostat and lowered the temperature. Once up to her office, I took a quick look at her Rolodex and found the combination to her small safe. There was a folder that contained her will. I was surprised that I inherited the house and some of her other assets. Some money was left to Sheila Turney and smaller amounts to various charities and organizations. The rest of her assets were given to the spiritualist camp and its board of trustees. I wondered if I should contest that part of the will given that she was writing an exposé on the church and camp. She apparently had not taken the time to change her will. Her will also indicated that she wanted to be cremated.

Given all that was going on and particularly our conversation at dinner, I decided it was important to look into this spiritualist camp.

My computer search engine brought up a number of references to a spiritualist camp called Cassadaga. In 1894, George

P. Colby, known as the "seer of spiritualism," bought some land in northeastern Florida and invited some of his followers to join him. Over the years, the small village known as Cassadaga slowly expanded, with followers building houses on lots sold by the camp.

In the early 1900s, some of Colby's followers became unhappy with how he was running the camp and particularly with the teachings at his church. This splinter group of spiritualists bought a piece of land north of Vero Beach and set up the Spiritual and Health Camp. Psychic mediums, spiritual healers, and preachers came to the camp that became known by some as a second "village of devils."

I needed to find out more about the camp. A quick look at their webpage provided a good deal of information. I discovered that spiritualism is a science, a philosophy, and a religion. Classes were offered—for a price—on mediumship development, ancient wisdom, and séances. People were invited to join various groups studying the occult. I was puzzled that my aunt would be so interested in any of this, but I've found that people often take different routes to fulfill their spiritual needs. It also surprised me that Aunt Elsie had never spent much time discussing this part of her life with me given the fact that she was so very generous to the camp in her will. But then again, I am someone who is not the least interested in so-called spiritual matters. I believe in things I can see, touch, and feel with my hands. Maybe she decided that talking to me about the camp and mysticism would be a waste of time. If so, she was right. Perhaps she was a bit embarrassed by her interest and belief in spirits.

Back to the practical world—I talked to Sheila, who said she wanted to take care of the funeral arrangements and would like to arrange an open house at my aunt's home inviting a few friends, her book club, and some neighbors. I was happy to let her take on those tasks. But I also was happy to have some celebration of my aunt's life. She had achieved quite a bit, becoming a schoolteacher, a wife, and a well-known author. Surely she deserved a decent send-off from her friends. Besides, she was a very delightful person.

While I was at my aunt's house, I paid particular attention to the stairs. They were rather steep but had railings on both sides. There was no carpeting on the steps, and they were fairly wide and reasonably easy to navigate. Given my aunt's relatively good health and her agility, I was a bit puzzled that she tripped at the top of the stairs where there was nothing to trip on. But accidents do happen, and most are just that—accidents.

CHAPTER SIX

THE NEPHEW BECOMES THE DETECTIVE

I live in a rather modest townhouse on Cardinal Drive, in Vero Beach, a bit over one block from the beach. The house is close to the main shopping area on the barrier island, within walking distance of several good restaurants and a number of specialty stores selling high-end goods to both well-off locals and tourists. The island is the location of several high-end developments showcasing million-dollar houses. I am a patron of the restaurants and the stores that sell pastries but do not frequent the clothing or jewelry stores. There wasn't a real grocery store on the island, so every week or so I went to the Publix in town.

My routine was to take a walk north on the beach and stop at a coffee shop, take my coffee outdoors to drink it on the patio, and make my way back home. I spent my time writing, reading, and I will admit to regularly napping. Evenings were pretty routine—either a trip to a brewery close by, or a glass or two of wine and a homemade meal out on the patio at home and a bit of television. Not a very exciting life but a pleasant one.

I did have a great neighbor in the townhouse next to mine—Trudy. She was a longtime resident of Vero Beach, specifically Rio Mar, a high-end group of residences surrounding the Rio Mar golf club. Established in the '20s, Rio Mar was an enclave of old money. Trudy lived there for fifty-odd years and knew everyone in the area and in Vero Beach. She was sort of a small-town Gertrude Stein, knowing everybody and holding court at her home. She moved to the townhouse when her home in Rio Mar, just around the corner, became a bit too much to maintain.

Trudy and I had become close friends, and I depended on her social knowledge of the town for all the current gossip and news. Trudy was in her nineties and very sharp. She was very well read and had an incredible memory. Besides, she was fun to be around.

We just hit it off well together. I told Trudy about my aunt's accident as well as my concerns about it. She thought my worries about my aunt's death seemed reasonable and said, "Keep me informed about what you are doing. This sounds like a good case for a former detective to pursue."

I did go to the open house arranged by Sheila and picked up my aunt's ashes from the funeral home. It was sad to see such a vibrant person reduced to ashes and bits of bone in a vase. I could not remember if my aunt was a Christian who believed in the afterlife. After the funeral, I thought my life would return to its normal boring routine. Was I wrong?

One afternoon, sitting in my office at home, I got a call from Aunt Elsie's book agent Gloria Cousins.

"I have been talking with your aunt's publisher, and the two of us decided to ask you to finish her book. If that works out, we would like you to continue the series. We know about your book of short stories and believe that another McKenzie would be the perfect person to carry on."

My first reaction was to say that I did not want to commit myself to such an arrangement. I was not sure that I had the talent, the patience, or the interest. The agent, Gloria, was not going to be discouraged easily.

"Think about it, and perhaps even look at Elsie's unfinished draft and then call me back in a couple of days. That is the least that you could do. Remember, you would be carrying on a tradition."

I agreed to do what she asked, saying, "I will be in touch, although I am not at all sure I am up to such a task." After some encouraging words, she made sure I had her telephone number and gave me her address again.

Despite my initial negative reaction, I thought about little except the agent's offer over the next day or so. I even mentioned the proposal to my neighbor, Trudy. She said, "It's a great opportunity. I think you should accept. Perhaps you will become a famous author and even make a little money that you can spend on me. A dinner or two would be fine."

I met Trudy over ten years ago, when she asked me to join a writers group that had met at her house each Monday for years. A variety of people attended; some had published books, others were writing memoirs, and others were planning to write something. While in the writing group, I wrote short stories that I read to the group each Monday. I began to really enjoy it and developed a particular style, writing very short stories with rather surprising endings. I started by writing the first few sentences of the story and then the last two sentences. The middle was filled in later. After writing stories for several years, I decided to find an agent and a publisher. A book of short stories was the result.

I grew very fond of Trudy, and when she needed to move from her old residence in Rio Mar, I told her about a townhouse that was for sale next to my place. She bought the house, and we continued to enjoy each other's company. Trudy was my entry into Vero Beach society; she often asked me to accompany her to various gatherings and cocktail parties.

When I visited Trudy's home to attend the writers group, her cat Charles seemed to take a special interest in me—often lying against my leg or on top of my shoes. Now, I always wondered why a female cat was named Charles.

After Trudy moved next to me, Charles, if I was around, would spend afternoons lying contentedly on my patio, much to Trudy's displeasure initially. But as Trudy and I became better acquainted, she did not mind and in fact encouraged Charles to "watch over" me. Trudy often told me that Charles, who was somewhat larger than most cats and had a mangy yellow coat and a brush of white hair around her nose, had a sixth sense to befriend good people who were lonely. I never thought of myself as lonely, but I guess I appeared to be that to someone as gregarious as Trudy. According to Trudy, Charles also had the unique ability to sort out the kind and thoughtful people from those whose instincts ran in the opposite direction. He would rub up against people in the first category and shy away from the others.

Trudy's encouragement helped me make up my mind about finishing my aunt's novel. I had read some of her novels and enjoyed them. They were not too complex and usually had engaging, well-plotted storylines with an unexpected twist or two. Maybe I could pick up where she left off and at the very least complete the unfinished novel to keep her series of books alive. I decided to take a look at Elsie's computer and read through the current draft. The idea of working on the novel became more and more intriguing as I thought about it. My life was a bit boring, and I always could use some additional money. Besides, what if I really had a bestseller? Maybe it would be made into a movie, and I would become famous as Trudy had suggested.

CHAPTER SEVEN

ELSIE'S FILES

Opening the front door of my aunt's house was a jolt. I again needed to lower the air conditioning. I found the controls and then headed up to her office. The desktop computer was a Mac, a model I was familiar with. Looking in her Rolodex, I found her password; I already knew her email address. It was easy to locate the unfinished draft. I emailed a copy to my computer so I could read what she had written at home rather than have to come back to her house.

While in the office, I went through some paper files to see if there was anything that might be helpful with stepping into Elsie's shoes as an author. I did find a file containing the contract for the new book and another labeled "Collaborator and Investigator—Alan Brooks." That file was a bit odd, and I put it and the contract in my briefcase. I also found a file labeled "Spiritualist Camp" and added it to the other material.

When I got home, I looked at the contract. It was fairly straightforward, with percentages going to the agent, the editor, the publisher, and an Alan Brooks, whoever that was. There was a note in the file indicating that Elsie had made about $90,000 after expenses on her previous book. Pretty good considering an article I'd recently read on the "profits" of fiction writers. For a known writer, profits averaged just under $100,000.

Why was Alan Brooks getting a percentage? The question was answered in the paperwork. Brooks had been involved in most of Elsie's books as a technical advisor.

There were several folders containing information on the spiritualist camp and the church. My aunt apparently was deeply involved with mysticism. I thought I knew my aunt well, but I certainly had missed this aspect of her life.

I needed to get myself organized rather than scurrying from one idea to the next like a head with its chicken cut off. I decided to write down what I needed to do with some sense of order and priority. I had found that making lists of what I needed to do as well as keeping track of interviews was something that served me well when I was a working detective.

First, I needed to find Alan Brooks and talk with him.

Second, I needed to find out what my aunt was currently working on, who would want to change what she was writing, and why.

Third, I needed to read my aunt's draft novel, the one she had stopped writing, and plan how to complete it.

Fourth, I should read some of her published novels to get a better idea of her style and some sense of how she went about the task of writing a novel.

Fifth, I had to tell the agent and publisher that I would complete the novel.

A lot to do!

CHAPTER EIGHT

ELSIE'S COLLABORATOR

Alan Brooks's address was in my aunt's Rolodex. What would I do without that device? He lived in the nearby town of Fort Pierce. That was about an hour drive from Vero, so off I went using the car's map system to get me to the address.

I drove down Indian River Road, past the circle, and turned onto the second street on the right. The house was a small but very neat rambler set back from the road. After parking in the driveway, I went up to the front door and knocked. A small middle-aged woman with rather startlingly white hair answered the door. Maybe she was more than middle aged.

"How can I help you?" she asked rather timidly.

"I am looking for Alan Brooks. He was a friend of my aunt Elsie McKenzie who recently died in an accident in her home. I wanted to talk with him about my aunt."

The woman said, "I am Alan's cousin and am taking care of the house for him. He has been in an assisted living home since his accident a few months ago. Alan talked about working with Elsie McKenzie. She was an author I believe. He apparently had known her for years, working as some sort of consultant. He will be upset to learn of her death."

We talked some about Alan, the fact that he had been a police detective. She gave me the address of the home where he was now living. It was across from the Indian State River College, and my GPS took me there without error.

I always went into nursing homes with considerable apprehension. The people in them always looked to be more than a little dazed. Many with breathing machines or carrying oxygen bottles and some in wheelchairs or using walkers. I knew many would never get out alive and that they knew it. It was very depressing. Maybe I was afraid I would end up in a similar facility. After visiting one of these facilities I always thought about how I would rather put an end to my life by taking poison or an overdose of something rather than end up in one. Seemed like a good choice, but time crept up on you before you knew it. Then it was too late to take any rational action.

After asking at the desk for Alan Brooks, I was directed to a gentleman sitting in a wheelchair watching television. He was quite thin but seemed alert and when he noticed me coming toward him gave me a friendly smile. His white hair was neatly combed, and he had shaved carefully. Wearing a bright Hawaiian shirt and khaki trousers, he looked pretty sharp.

"Mr. Brooks, my name is Robert McKenzie. I am Elsie McKenzie's nephew. I've been told that you knew her quite well? I'm sorry to tell you that she died in an accident in her home. And I am trying to make contact with some of her friends."

I could see that Alan did not know of Elsie's death. His expression changed, and I could almost see tears forming.

"I am so sorry to hear of her death. She was a good friend and colleague for many years."

"How did you meet her?"

He thought for a moment and said, "I first met her at a conference of mystery writers. The conference was held at a spiritualist camp. My background was in law enforcement, and I had been asked to give a talk at the conference on the subjects of policing and working as a detective."

"So it turned into a long-term arrangement?"

"Elsie and I struck it off well, and she ultimately asked if I would help her as a consultant in my area of expertise. We worked out an agreement where I would get a small percentage of the profit from her books, and she was able to call me with specific questions as she wrote." He scrutinized me a bit. "There was nothing unusual in our relationship. Purely business. No hanky panky."

I said, "I am surprised that my aunt never mentioned her arrangement with you. We talked quite a bit about her writing and various problems she encountered, but the subject of having an expert advising her never came up."

Alan said, "I am not surprised. Authors sometimes do not want people to know that they look widely for expertise. Maybe she wanted to be seen as the expert. Although when we were with other authors she never seemed reluctant to introduce me and explain how I helped her. I found her a very open and supportive person. She took advice easily and always seemed to appreciate it."

Alan told me he had broken a hip in a fall at his house. He said it was an unusual accident because he was usually very careful going down steps. But as he was walking down his backdoor steps, he tripped on something and fell. He said it was puzzling because after the accident he could not find anything that he could have tripped on. According to him it was more like someone tripped him, but no other person was present.

We spent considerable time talking about his friendship and business connection with Elsie. He clearly was very fond of her and described how the arrangement worked. "We were regularly in contact over some detail about how the police conducted an investigation or even such odd things as how loan sharks and ordinary criminals operated," Alan said.

"Although she never wrote about serial killers, she often asked about how their minds worked. I had investigated a couple murders that I thought were the work of a serial killer but never helped catch them. Others in other states caught up with them. I too was intrigued by them. Elsie thought they were just evil. I attributed their deadly compulsions and the need to feed these compulsions to a screw being loose."

I pointed out that I was a former detective working in Denver. He nodded as if he were aware of that fact. Alan was particularly interested that I had investigated and helped apprehend a man who the FBI considered to be a serial killer.

"At the time," I said, "I was amazed at the craftiness of the killer."

Alan was aware that nearly all serial killers are men. He also was aware that they usually killed for the sheer pleasure of killing.

"What intrigued me," I said, "was the way they went about their killings usually was almost ritualistic."

"Probably why Elsie thought serial killers were evil," Alan said.

It was enjoyable exchanging stories about incidents we had been involved in when we worked as detectives, even if they were somewhat gruesome. Our common experiences were a bonding, and soon we were talking as if old friends.

Alan had started as a patrol officer, walking a beat in Fort Pierce, a town south of Vero Beach, and worked his way up to detective. He said he had spent over twenty-five years as a policeman and enjoyed the experience. When he retired, he was a bit young to stop working and decided to become a private detective. Soon after Alan and Elsie met at the conference involving mystery writers, Alan said Elsie contacted him to ask some questions about police work. That conversation led to his working for Elsie as a consultant, helping her with some technical information on policing and police procedures.

We both had experience with fraud cases. I said, "Denver even had a bunco squad that investigated the full range of scams. It looked into everything from people who promised work on a house only to take the down payment and hit the road to fraudulent stock offerings."

Alan asked, "Did you ever have a case involving fortune tellers or seers?"

I said, "I could not remember one, but it did seem to me that it was not a crime for someone to offer advice even if it involved the 'spirits.' If someone was willing to pay for that advice no matter how useless it was, I could not see how it broke the law."

Alan said, "I did some work for your aunt at her request on the local fortune tellers in the Vero area. I will pull out my report from my files and give it to you. It was an interesting investigation but only proved the point that you just made—'buyer beware,' but it is not a crime to read someone's fortune."

At that point, I raised my concerns about my aunt's death and mentioned some of the anomalies. How she fell head first, which usually did not happen when someone tripped and fell. The fact that, for her age, Elsie was very agile. We agreed that her death seemed a bit unusual.

Alan said, "Before my fall, your aunt had complained that the text of her new book, an exposé, was being changed without her permission. I told her that the only person who could be changing her writing was her editor."

Alan also expressed some puzzlement about my aunt's apparent strong interest in the occult. He said Elsie was a regular at her book club and told Alan about conversations she had with some of the members of the club about spiritualism and the camp. One of the members told her that she regularly went to the camp and was very enthusiastic about the mediums and their vision of the future. She told Elsie that she had been in contact with her dead father and also had gotten some information indicating she would make a considerable amount of money by investing in a high-end property development company in Vero Beach. Another member of the book club had indicated she also had been advised to invest in this particular company by a medium at the camp. Alan said my aunt became suspicious of the mediums and their predictions and decided to look into what was going on at the camp.

Alan said my aunt subsequently made a trip to the camp to see for herself what was going on there. When my aunt checked into the inn that was part of the spiritual camp, he said, she made several appointments with mediums, visited with some of the managers of the inn, and spent some time at the church. Elsie provided Alan with a rather complete readout of her activities and her judgment of what was going on at the camp. She thought the mediums were using their special positions to influence people to invest in projects that would benefit the camp. She concluded that people at the camp suspected she intended to expose these activities.

"I could not understand her interest in spiritualism, but it seemed to be a constant in her life and her writing," he said. "She was interested in what people told her about being pressured to invest in companies. I think she also had invested some money in either the church or some scheme involving the camp and the church. But she was never specific about what she had done or how much she had given the church."

Alan said my aunt had asked him to go with her when she made another visit.

"She wanted to talk to some of the spiritualists and spend some time at the church. She thought I might help her. I did go with her, and we spent several days talking to people and just nosing around. She spent considerable time talking to both staff and visitors to the church."

Alan talked about what he did during his visit to the inn. Apparently Elsie had asked him to talk to people about their experiences with the mediums in the church. Elsie told Alan she was looking for any evidence that their "predictions" involved getting money from their "clients."

"I spent a few days at the inn chatting up people—primarily middle-aged or older women," he said. "Some of those I talked with mentioned their mediums had indicated that they would come into some money or make a good investment in the near future. There was also some reference to giving money to the church or keeping the church in their will. But none of this was apparently done with any great pressure, and it was just part of the pitch."

CHAPTER NINE

THE BARTENDER TALKS

Alan mentioned a particularly interesting conversation he had late one night sitting at the bar and talking to Ben the bartender.

When asked how good the mediums were at predicting the future, the bartender said, "It is not surprising that the 'seers' have insight into their customers. They do a lot of preparation." That struck Alan as sort of odd.

"When I asked what the bartender meant by 'preparation,' Ben responded by saying that when people made reservations at the inn they were asked for their email address. Someone on the camp staff followed up, looking at Facebook and other information on that individual. That information was made available to the various mediums that might end up having a session with that particular guest. Again, I thought, nothing illegal, but somewhat beyond merely reading palms."

The bartender asked Alan if he and his lady friend who accompanied him were reporters or writers because they were asking a lot of questions. Ben told Alan, "You should be careful because people trying to dig up dirt on the church or the mediums have had bad experiences." Alan told him that he was not a reporter or writing about the camp but asked what he meant by "bad experiences." Ben appeared to be reluctant to say anything and then admitted that a couple of people who recently came to the camp with the intention of writing a story exposing the whole idea of spiritualism were killed in a car accident shortly after they were asked to leave. He said there were other examples in the past, but he had no direct knowledge of them.

Alan said Ben ended the conversation saying in a hushed voice, "The spirits look after their own."

I told Alan I would like to spend some more time talking about his visit to the camp and church and what he uncovered, but I had to go back to Vero for an appointment. I said I would come back and talk with him again if that was okay. He indicated that he would get his notes about his visit to camp and his investigation into local fortune tellers and be ready to talk with me about everything he had done to help Elsie.

As I was leaving, he said, "You know that the house she bought in Vero Beach had some association with the occult. The next time you go to the house, walk into the backyard and look up at the second story."

He did not expand on the thought.

I left the meeting with Alan with more questions than answers. Driving back to Vero, I thought about my list. I changed and added to my list of things that I needed to follow up on:

FIRST: Look at my aunt's files for information on the house and spend some time looking at her camp file. Clearly this needed careful scrutiny.

SECOND: Talk with my aunt's agent and editor. They are the only people who had access to her draft, unless someone entered her house.

THIRD: Get busy reading the rest of her draft novel and look at some of her earlier novels. See if that provided some information about her concerns.

FOURTH: Decide whether or not to finish my aunt's draft novel.

CHAPTER TEN

A HOUSE WITH A HISTORY

Attacking the first thing on my list, I drove to Aunt Elsie's house the next day, went up to her office, found the file cabinet, and began going through it. Fortunately, she was a well-organized person. She seemed to have a file for every aspect of her life, and each file was clearly identified. It was easy to find a file with "House" on the label.

Elsie had purchased her house in what was called the Osceola Park over twenty years ago. She apparently had gotten into a bidding war over buying the house and had to raise her offer above the original offering. Elsie later found out that someone from the spiritual camp had been bidding against her. One note in the file indicated that my aunt had received an anonymous letter informing her that she should not buy the house and would regret it if she did. There also were several letters in the file sent over the course of a few years asking her to sell the house. All were from people associated with the camp. She had made a note on one of the letters indicating she had responded asking them to quit pestering her about selling the house.

The Osceola Park development where the house was located dated back to the early 1930s. It was composed of what were called cottages, primarily one-story houses of mixed style with an occasional two-story house, all placed along tree-lined avenues. Today some of the homes were bed and breakfasts or businesses.

My aunt's house was built in the mid to late 1930s. The builder was a man who moved from the camp to work with his uncle managing a large orange grove. There were several owners, and all seemed to have connections to the camp. Elsie had done some extensive remodeling, but the basic structure remained unchanged.

Remembering what Alan Brooks said, I went out into the backyard and looked up at the house. There was a door on the second story that seemed to have no purpose. It opened out to nothing but air. Maybe there had been steps once, but there was currently no evidence of any connection to the door. I had no idea when the door was put in place or why.

I went back in the house and immediately went up to the second floor and into the back bedroom. There it was—the door to nothing. The door was unlocked but hardly a security problem, at least from an outside intruder. As I opened the door, there was a rasping sound. Someone had nailed an insulation strip along the bottom of the door and it dragged noisily across the floor. You could see marks on the floor indicating that the door had been opened before.

Looking through the "House" file, I saw several newspaper clippings. Some of these mentioned the history of the house and included articles about spirits living in the house. Several people who lived nearby had reported hearing strange noises at night and seeing apparitions. They also reported that they could hear things being moved around—chairs and other furniture—when the house was not occupied. The house got a reputation of being haunted. There also was an article on what was described as the "door to nowhere." The purpose of the door was to allow spirits to enter or leave the house at will. I wondered if the spirits did not like knocking on the front door and bothering the inhabitants.

The mysteries surrounding my aunt were getting deeper and deeper.

CHAPTER ELEVEN

THE PLOT THICKENS

I decided that my next task would be to talk with my aunt's agent and her editor. Again I went to the Rolodex. I found Gloria Cousins, my aunt's agent, and her telephone number. I had misplaced it after her call. I called and said I would like to come to visit her and my aunt's editor. Both lived in Kissimmee, a town about two hours' drive north of Vero. Gloria said she would be happy to talk with me and was still interested in having me finish the book. We set a time later in the week.

It was a pleasant drive up Highway 95 then onto Highway 41. Kissimmee is a small town that sooner or later would be absorbed into greater Orlando. I found Gloria's house and met with her and my aunt's editor.

Although they were not related, my aunt's agent and editor could be easily mistaken as sisters. Both were middle-aged with graying hair. They dressed alike and seemed to finish each other's sentences. I enjoyed talking with them. They were very pleasant, clearly liked my aunt, and were willing to discuss any issue quite frankly.

After some discussion about my aunt and her books, I told them that my aunt had been concerned that her text was being changed by some unknown force. I said that I knew that she regularly sent pieces of her draft to them and wondered if they knew anything about the changes that seemed to concern her so much. The editor, Jane Smallwell, said she regularly recommended changes to the text but never made them final without my aunt's agreement. Gloria said she never got very involved in the text of the novels unless she had a major problem with the story.

Jane had been unusually quiet while I was talking to Gloria. Finally, looking directly at me, she said my aunt had stopped work on her current novel to begin something entirely new.

"If the novel was going so well, why did she want to put it on hold?"

Jane said, "Your aunt felt a compulsion to begin a new book. It was to be an exposé on spiritualism. It was this new piece or the outline of it that your aunt claimed was being changed—not the draft novel Gloria, the publisher, and I am asking you to finish."

Jane said she noticed some changes were being made to the new book in the evening and that was a bit surprising given that Elsie usually wrote in the morning and early afternoon. It appeared, she said, that several large chunks had been removed.

"Were the changes being made by my aunt?" I asked.

"It would be difficult to determine who actually made the changes," Jane said. "I was a bit concerned about what was happening and asked your aunt about it. She seemed a bit worried and uncertain but did not have an answer. She did say that the changes were also being made on her computer as well. She told me that she would work out the problem and left it at that."

Before leaving, Gloria asked me if I had decided to finish the novel. She was very pleased when I responded in the affirmative. I told her that I thought my aunt would want me to do that. And for me, it would be a way of honoring her memory. Gloria said she would prepare the necessary contract and send it to me.

I left Gloria's house more confused than when I had arrived. I was gathering information, but it only further confused the situation. I decided that my next task would be to read the unfinished draft of my aunt's novel and then look at the outline of the new book to see if it offered any clues as to what was going on in her mind and what changes had actually been made to her text.

CHAPTER TWELVE

THE UNFINISHED NOVEL

I opened my computer and began reading the unfinished novel. Although I had read Elsie's books as they were published, I now read the new novel in an attempt to understand her writing style, how storylines developed and how characters were created. At the same time, I needed to pick up on the story and complete it. I read what my aunt had written thinking how I might add to or modify it.

The novel started with a small lie, a white lie. And that was the title of the book, *The White Lie*:

> His wife Jane hectored him to visit an old friend who was ill and, she believed, needed company. John was reluctant to visit Fred, because he was terribly boring and would not stop talking about stupid things. John told his wife that he stopped to visit Fred, but in reality, he had wandered around Vero Beach doing various tasks and just wasting time.

The problem was that Fred was later found dead in his house, murdered the same morning as John's fabricated visit. John told several others about the visit as well as his wife. When the police subsequently interviewed him, John decided to stick with the story about visiting Fred. That made him a person of interest in the investigation.

There was an investigation of the crime scene, background checks on Fred, and the usual search for evidence. The evidence found appeared to single out Fred as the most likely suspect.

The main theme was a person telling a white lie and then being caught up in a web of their own making. Fred, although innocent, is identified in a newspaper article as a person of interest in the murder. He is a well-known lawyer in town and because of the publicity begins to lose his clients. His wife Jane moves out of their house. His life is ruined.

The draft came to a rather sudden end with a note from my aunt in parentheses that read: *(I have decided to stop work on this story and begin a totally new book that involves a fraudulent spiritual church and phony fortune tellers.)*

I thought I could finish the novel and improve it along the way. But first I decided to find out what my aunt had discovered about the spiritual camp and determine if that had any connection with her death. That had priority over finishing the novel.

I found the draft of her new book on the computer and opened it. I was a bit surprised by the content. It was not a narrative but an outline and detailed notes my aunt had collected on the spiritual camp. The information was laid out very systematically and included the following major topics:

History of the Camp
Management Structure
Key people running the village
The Church and its management
Finances of the village and Church
Mediums
Background and Facebook info
People who had joined and left the flock
Interviews of disenchanted

There was considerable information under each heading. My aunt had done an impressive job of gathering data. If anyone in a leadership position at the camp got access to her notes, they would be very concerned about the information becoming public. One footnote was particularly interesting. It read: *Ask Alan to review the monthly newsletter from the camp, which regularly mentioned donations to the church and camp. Pay particular attention to anyone who died unexpectedly after donating.*

There also was a note that indicated she was no longer putting information on the camp onto her computer because it was being tampered with. She decided to record by handwritten notes. Looking in my aunt's files, I found one labeled "Notes on the Camp." But it was empty.

CHAPTER THIRTEEN

ATTEMPT TO VISIT ALAN AGAIN

I thought the next step in this process should be to get back in touch with Alan Brooks and find out what he knew about my aunt's interest in the cult and their visit to the camp. I had told him that I wanted to talk with him again.

I called the nursing home to make an appointment to visit with Alan Brooks. After being shuffled among several people, I finally ended up with the manager of the home, Mrs. Adams. She informed me in a sad voice that Alan had died. I asked for some details about his death, and she said it would be better if I came to the nursing home to talk rather than do this over the phone. I made an appointment with Mrs. Adams for that afternoon.

Driving back to Fort Pierce and the nursing home, I thought about my earlier talk with Alan. He had told me about my aunt's concerns about the church, gave me some history of her house, and mentioned that he had gone to the camp with her on an "investigative" trip. I should have followed up on his memories of what was uncovered at that time rather than putting it off. I wondered what he could have told me.

The group gathered around in the main room of the nursing home had not changed, except Alan was not sitting in the wheelchair watching television. I found the office of the home manager and told the secretary I had an appointment with Mrs. Adams. A few minutes later, a middle-aged woman with long, graying hair came out of her office to greet me. She expressed her sadness about the death of Alan and asked me to come into her office.

After some conversation about her sadness over Alan, she very cautiously began to talk about the circumstances surrounding his death. Alan fell down the steps leading down from the large deck that stretched across the back of the building. An autopsy showed that he died from a broken neck and head injuries. It was a bit puzzling because Alan was still using the wheelchair, and it seemed unlikely that he would have tried to negotiate the steps. His wheelchair was set at the top of the steps with the brake locked. A caregiver said she saw Alan walking very cautiously around the deck. She saw him standing at the top of the stairs. She said that all of a sudden, he raised his arms as if he was startled. He then fell down the steps.

Mrs. Adams apparently was very upset because of Alan's death and the questions it raised about security and safety at the rehab facility. Apparently Alan frequently went on the deck, but she could think of no reason why Alan would stand at the top of the steps. Alan was doing well recovering from his hip injury but not well enough to attempt the steps. She thought he probably would have been able to leave the facility and return home in a week or so.

As I was leaving, Mrs. Adams called me back and handed me a large envelope she said was found in Alan's personal effects. It was addressed to me.

CHAPTER FOURTEEN

NOTES FROM ALAN

Once home, I immediately opened the envelope. Inside was an investigator's notebook with a detailed record of Alan's visit to the spiritualist camp. I looked through the notes and found a clear summary of what Alan already had told me. It did add some new information about why my aunt originally got started on the exposé of the camp. It also provided detail on her visit to the camp. Perhaps most interesting, the package contained a rather detailed description of how my aunt became interested in the occult.

Case: Spiritualism and Elsie McKenzie—Alan Brooks
August 9

Elsie asked me to investigate the spiritual camp or commune, which includes a church and an inn. Elsie said she had been associated with the spiritualist camp for several years. In fact, the house she bought some years ago had been the longtime residence of one of the people who ran the camp. Elsie said she first became interested in spiritualism after her husband, Albert, died. She had always meditated in one form or another, but once Albert died, she needed to mediate an hour or so every night to ease her loneliness. One night while meditating, she said, a deep darkness seemed to engulf her. She felt someone or something was trying to communicate with her. She invited that "presence" to enter into her and felt a great feeling of calm and peace. But weeks later, no matter how much she sought that same "presence," it did not come again.

Elsie said she had heard about a spiritualist camp nearby and that each Wednesday night, a "seer" conducted séances during which the seer contacted "those on the other side" who might be willing or able to communicate with the living. Elsie said she could attend the church where the séances were conducted, paying a fee for each séance. The church did not promise that a "spiritual contact" would occur. It depended on whether those on the "other side" wanted to speak with her or not. Elsie said she attended three séances before the "presence," which turned out to be her husband, Albert, spoke to her. For the last several years, Elsie said, she has been attending a séance almost every week. Usually, Albert only communicated with her about once a month.

Elsie had always written novels but with only moderate success. But Albert's communications proved to be a boon to her novel writing. He would not only instruct her on the title of the book, but also sometimes would list the chapters and sketch out some chapters for her. Soon her books were bringing in hundreds of dollars each month. Elsie was able to reduce the mortgage on her house with her earnings. Last year she was able to pay off the mortgage. Although I had collaborated on a few novels with Elsie, I knew nothing about Albert's involvement "from the other side." My job was to research the location of the novels and provide what Elsie called "the local color." I also would write up conversations I had with locals in the towns in which her novels were located, which she incorporated into the novels.

As a detective I am sort of a black-and-white, factual sort. I had heard about séances but never attended one and never wanted to attend one. I asked Elsie why she wanted me to investigate. She said she had been troubled over the last year or so since the new woman, Abigale Cruz, took over as head of the church. She thought perhaps a scam was taking place. The alleged scam had to do with a couple of the "seers." They apparently got information "from the other side" instructing generally little old ladies on which stocks to invest in. The seers then suggested if the stocks brought in a windfall they might show their gratitude by donating a portion to the church.

August 15–17

I spent the last two days as a guest at the inn. Most of the guests were older, and as I made polite conversation with them during mealtime, they talked about the séances they had attended. Some came from as far away as Los Angeles. Most wanted to communicate with children, siblings, or parents who "were on the other side." A couple from New York had heard that "the other side" sometimes provided excellent investment suggestions. The innkeeper, Leroy Headly, asked several times why I was staying at the inn, since I seemed to have little interest in attending the séances or the church. Headly, about forty-five, looked like an ex-bouncer at some local pub. I did a Google search on him, but nothing came up. I never mentioned my connection to Elsie, but the second day after lunch, Headly asked me if I knew Elsie.

August 24

At Elsie's insistence I attended the church service, which began around 7 p.m. I am not a church-going type. But this was like no church service I ever attended. After some Bible reading by Abigale Cruz and some announcements, the congregation just went into sort of a group mediation until someone spoke up and said "the other side" is present and then spoke in an odd language that others referred to as tongues.

Abigale is quite the package. About forty or so but looking much younger, with flaming red hair, cream-colored skin, and a seductive voice. What was startling for me is that two of those attending the church later told me "the other side" warned the church that some of those attending the service might want to do harm. I was expecting my name to come up.

The service ended around 9 p.m. After everyone left, I went back to my car and waited around to see if anything else took place. About 11:30 p.m. some twelve guests at the inn came over to the church. I got out of my car and went around back of the church. The door was locked, but I got it opened and quietly moved inside. A few moments later around midnight, Abigale appeared. She instructed all twelve of those attending to take off their clothes. She then took off her clothes. Although somewhat shocked, I enjoyed the sight. She then explained that all the naked people should join hands in a circle and move clockwise.

She said the spirits above would then move counterclockwise. This, she said, would create the "gyre" in which the spirits above could become connected to those moving clockwise. Abigale then began to hum and sing in a beautiful voice. About thirty or so minutes later, Abigale stopped and began speaking in a voice that was detached and definitely a man's voice. She barked out that everyone should stop moving. "Someone is here who does not belong," Abigale shouted. The twelve naked people became somewhat agitated. I quickly moved back to the door I had unlocked and quietly returned to my car and drove off.

August 25

I met with Elsie this afternoon and explained what I had witnessed the night before, after the church service. Elsie appeared to be shocked. I asked her if she had ever attended a midnight gathering in the church. She said no, but I don't know if I believe her. She then said I should not go to the camp again. That it might be dangerous. Elsie then explained that the exposé she was writing was being changed each night. I asked what she meant by "changed." She said her discussion about the investment instructions to church members disappeared and the suggestion from church leadership that donation to the church be increased was deleted. I thought about this, and my conclusion was that Elsie might have made those changes herself on some subconscious level but did not remember doing so. Perhaps she was imagining all this.

* * *

Alan's report of what he witnessed at the camp and at the midnight ceremony caused me to reflect on my spiritual beliefs as well as trying to understand Elsie's. I was raised Roman Catholic, but when my mother died early in my life, I stopped going to church except to attend funerals or accompany friends at Christmas or Easter.

Alan continued to write about things my aunt asked him to do. For example, she wanted some research on psychics and mediums in the Vero Beach area. Alan wrote: *I don't know whether this was background for the book she was writing on the Spiritual and Health Camp or for some other book. In any case, I provided the following report to your aunt about two months ago.*

CHAPTER FIFTEEN

PSYCHICS AND MEDIUMS IN VERO BEACH

Using my Mac, I found there are some twenty-five businesses that are listed under the heading of "fortune tellers" in the Vero Beach online directory.

I looked at each of the establishments listed and can found the following information:

- All except three listed women as the proprietor; two identified men and the third referred to a "team."
- Most advertised themselves as psychics, mediums, and spiritual consultants.
- Nearly all indicated they do readings and consultations for relationships and careers. Most do tarot card reading and some refer to past life regression.

Of the twenty-five I reviewed, most had been in the business for a considerable period—thirty to fifty years. There were only four that had spent less than ten years as fortune tellers.

Looking at the reviews provided by the businesses in their advertisements, I found that many customers thanked them for the "love spells" they provided. A few reviews mentioned good advice given on career choices.

I directly contacted several of the businesses listed in the directory but was careful to use a burner phone and not reveal any true information about myself. I decided that if I had to pay I would do so by cash or a money order rather than credit card or check.

My pitch on several calls was that I wanted to get in touch with my wife who had passed away just a few months earlier. When she died there were several unresolved issues between us, and I wanted to get past them.

I had a friendly conversation with a couple of people who sounded like they could put me in touch with my dead wife. I asked about cost, and they seemed pretty evasive. It depended on the time and difficulty, and one suggested that I should initially pay for a half hour of their time—one hundred dollars. They indicated that contact such as I was asking for was not guaranteed and often took several sessions.

There was one further development, which left me very puzzled. I got an email from one of the people I had talked to about contacting my dead wife. I had not given my name nor had I contacted her through email. She said in her email that she wanted no further contact with me because she believed I was up to no good and was trying to do something that would harm her.

How had she found me? I had been very careful to leave no tracks and give no indication of my identity.

CHAPTER SIXTEEN

ALAN FINDS AN INTERESTING THREAD

There was another piece of paper in the material that Alan left for me. It was a letter addressed to Alan from one of the several "mediums" he had contacted in his investigation for my aunt. The letter described her contact with the leader of a spiritual camp near Vero. Apparently she had heard of Alan's "investigation" and had decided that she would contact him directly.

The letter began with a personal description of her background and long interest in spiritualism. She came from the West Coast and had been involved with a variety of what she described as "nutty people," primarily offbeat religious groups. She said California seemed to spawn strange beliefs and cited the Rosicrucians as one of several groups she belonged to. When she moved to Vero Beach, she found no familiar philosophical or religious groups. She discovered the Spiritual and Health Camp and became a regular attendee at readings and meditation groups. Going regularly to the camp, she found a comforting and peaceful environment. The letter went on to describe her volunteering with various committees at the camp and particularly her decision to begin generously contributing money to the camp. Things went well for a considerable period of time, and she became an accepted member of the church and community. When the new director was appointed, things began to change. She was pressured to increase her donations, and when she expressed some reluctance, she was, in her words, excommunicated from the church and the camp.

There were no other records in Alan's material. He had been a great source. I wished I had spent more time with him.

CHAPTER SEVENTEEN

LOOKING INTO SPIRITUALISM

After Alan Brooks died in such an unusual fashion, it dawned on me that perhaps Sheila Turney, who was my Aunt Elsie's best friend and discovered her body at the bottom of the stairs, might know something about Elsie's attraction to spiritualism.

It took me a couple of days to get in touch with Sheila. Her phone's answering service was always full when I called. Finally, I called around 9:30 at night. After about four rings, Sheila answered in a voice that sounded like I had awakened her. It took her a couple of minutes to remember who I was, but she agreed to have lunch with me in three days at Panera Bread. In my prior chauvinistic Denver life, I would have referred to Panera Bread as a fast-food chick eatery. But now enlightened, I referred to Panera Bread as a fast-food eatery for the other genders.

At about 11:35 a.m., I arrived at Panera Bread, got a cup of coffee, and found a booth in the back that was somewhat isolated. At 12:15, Sheila arrived. I left my cup of coffee on the table to stake out my possession and joined Sheila. I had met her a couple of times over the last four years, but she did not seem to recognize me until I introduced myself. She looked older than I recalled. Perhaps losing her best friend took something out of her, although she probably was seventy or so. She looked all of that. She ordered a Strawberry Poppyseed Salad and Chai Tea, and I ordered a Southwest Chile Lime Ranch Salad with Chicken, because it was the longest description of a salad I found. No one had taken my booth, although the eatery was packed. Women tend to be a lot more considerate than us males.

After some pleasantries, she began digesting her soup in earnest and only then began picking at her salad. I had already eaten my salad fare, so when she began eating bits of her salad, I asked if she was aware of my aunt's interest in spiritualism and the camp.

I noticed she squirmed a bit in the booth before saying, "Of course. I think I introduced her to the camp. Elsie was totally distressed when her husband, Albert, died. He was only in his late forties, if you recall. She did not have children, and you were in Denver. I was probably the only one around who she allowed to get close to her in her grief. She was a very private person and someone who thought she should be able to handle such things as her husband's death. But I saw she was becoming more and more depressed. She stopped writing novels. Ended going to church and even did not want to go out with me and other friends for dinner."

Sheila looked around to see if anyone might be listening to her before continuing. "I was the one who dabbled in spiritualism. I found that palmists at the camp accurately could describe earlier events in my life, and I enjoyed all the successful things they predicted. Some of which actually happened. I never had gone to a séance. But I thought it might help lift your aunt out of her depression."

Sheila looked at her empty chai tea cup. I took the hint and got up and ordered another. When I returned, I noticed Sheila had moved her chair closer to mine. Now in a softer voice, so she might not be overheard, she said, "I accompanied her to the camp and attended the séance with her. Both she and I were impressed with the spiritualist, a strikingly good-looking young man. He told Elsie how much Albert missed her and that Albert looked forward to being with her when she passed to the other side. He also reminded her about how much was in the insurance policy and accurately gave the amount she received. He was proud that he had arranged that for her. And now, come to think about it, he warned her about being careful when she was walking downstairs." Sheila's eyes began to tear. "I just thought of that. My, my."

"Did you go with her to other séances?" I asked.

"No, too spooky for me. But Elsie was hooked. And I was happy for her. The depression seemed to be lifted, and she began writing novels again."

Sheila was still tearing and thought we should end the meeting, but I had to ask one more question. "Did Aunt Elsie buy her home because it was previously owned by one of the founders of the camp?"

"You know I think that is what really gave validity to her attraction to the camp," she said. "She bought the house with the insurance money from Albert's untimely death. She thought Albert somehow arranged that from the other side. It strengthened her attraction to the camp."

Sheila opened her large purse and sought a yellow handy, then dabbed at her eyes and loudly blew her nose. "Sorry," she said, getting up from the booth. "I miss Elsie so much."

CHAPTER EIGHTEEN

MY RELIGIOUS EXPERIENCE

I was semi-raised in the Roman Catholic Church but over the last twenty years rarely went to services except sometimes with friends during Christmas or Easter. Reviewing what Alan Brooks wrote in his investigation, and especially the midnight service that took place at the church, was beyond anything I had ever heard of or thought about. I was way out of my league. I called a couple of my more religious friends and asked them if there was a priest in Vero Beach who they considered knowledgeable about communicating with dead people through mediums. They recommended Father Michael Yeats, a retired priest at St. Mary's.

Getting hold of Father Michael proved difficult. I was asked by the woman who answered the church telephone if I needed confession. I said I probably did, but that wasn't why I was calling Father Michael.

"The Father is semi-retired and rarely sees parishioners," the woman said. She asked if I attended St. Mary on a regular basis.

I lied and said, "Sometimes."

She then asked if I was snowbird. "No," I said. "I live here fulltime. I have for several years."

She then, in an accusatory voice, asked, "Are you a backsliding Catholic?"

I acknowledged the fact that church and I were not on the best of terms. "I was a police detective for a number of years," I said. "I've witnessed and was exposed to some of the worst elements of society. Difficult for me to believe in a God who permits that. I'm sorry."

Surprisingly, the woman's voice became friendly. "Oh, in that case, I am certain Father Michael would be glad to meet with you. He loves detectives and mystery books."

A couple of days later, this same woman called me and told me Father Michael would be willing to take a stroll with me the following Saturday.

"He walks four miles every morning," she said. "Meet him by the church office at 8 a.m. Don't be late because he will start walking without you. You know where the church is, don't you?"

I assured her that I knew where the church was. I arrived at the church, which was only a couple of blocks from my home, at 7:45 a.m. On the dot at 8 a.m., a short, white-haired, bow-legged man of about eighty appeared outside of the church office. He wore a sweater, even though the temperature was nearly eighty degrees, and a baseball cap that informed me he was a fan of the New York Yankees.

"You're the cop?" he asked by way of greeting. "My dad was a cop. Never made it up the ranks. Didn't want to kiss anybody's backside, you know."

I assured Father Michael I was retired because kissing backsides had become anathema to me, too. At that, Father Michael took off at a fast pace. As we walked, I began explaining about my Aunt Elsie's strange death and the strange death of her collaborator Alan Brooks. When I mentioned the spiritual camp, Father Michael made a gruff-like sound.

"Are you familiar with the camp?"

"Is the Pope Catholic?" he replied.

"I take it you've heard about it?" I said.

Father Michael stopped walking and looked at me suspiciously. I was aware of that look having been a detective for so long.

"It's been a thorn in my side for a number of years. Do you belong to the church at the camp?" he asked.

"No, no. That's why I'm here."

He grunted, looked at me again to see if I was telling the truth. I guess I passed the test because he started walking again. I quickly recounted the various comments made by Alan Brooks. Father Michael remained silent the entire time. Finally, after speaking and walking for twenty minutes or so, I tugged at Father Michael's arm, forcing him to stop walking.

"Father, does any of that make any sense?"

A bench near the beach was nearby. Father Michael nodded toward the bench that we should sit down.

"Son, I am aware of the séances that take place at the camp. I know a lot of people think they are harmless. I don't. Usually, people attend for two reasons. They miss their loved ones, like your aunt, or they need direction in their lives. They feel lost, and their lives seem to have no meaning. The camp takes advantage of these people. People who are suffering."

"What about the naked people moving clockwise in the church?" I asked.

Father Michael grabbed my arm with a force I could not believe he had in him.

"I never heard of that before."

"Do you think Alan Brooks made that up?" I asked.

Father Michael shook his head sadly.

"No. I think he wrote about what he saw. It's called a Black Mass. It is an attempt by those circling to be possessed by so-called demons on the other side. I assume most of those circling during the mass don't think they're inviting demons to enter into them. They think there are wise masters on the other side who will help them, give them advice. Make their lives a success."

I now shook my head. "Is that possible?"

"Son, I know this will sound strange to you," he began. "Most priests don't believe it even though they teach it. Few ministers I know believe it even though they preach it. The Bible tells us there are two types of angels. Dark angels and the glorious light angels of our Father. The dark angels are what many refer to as demons. Can they possess us? I don't know. What I do know is that they cannot possess us unless we invite them in. Like your aunt probably did."

Father Michael was quick to notice a certain fear that came over me.

"Don't be afraid," he said, touching my arm. "They can cause trouble to people, but even if you aren't a believer in Christ, they are limited in the damage they can do to you."

He got up and began walking back toward the church. As I caught up to him, he turned toward me and said, "I would be more concerned with the leaders of the camp. I would assume that if they were responsible for Mr. Brooks's death, they have something to hide and might be aware that your aunt has a nephew who used to be a detective."

We continued walking in silence until we were back at the church. "Wait here, son. I want to give you something."

A few minutes later, he presented me with a small wooden crucifix. "Keep this on you. If you feel there is a weird presence around you, lift it up toward the presence. It'll flee."

He turned and walked back to the church. As he opened the door, he looked back and said, "You'll be in my prayers. Perhaps you're the one to expose the evil at the camp like your aunt was trying to do."

CHAPTER NINETEEN

COMPLETING THE NOVEL

That evening I got a call from Gloria, my aunt's book agent, wanting to know what I had accomplished toward finishing the book. I was a bit embarrassed because in fact I had done nothing. I had been preoccupied with following up on my aunt's death.

I told Gloria that I had been totally involved in dealing with my aunt's estate and apologized for not getting to work on the novel. I said I would begin immediately and report my progress to her. I needed a break from worrying about my aunt's death, and the distraction of working on the book would be welcome.

Gloria said that in addition to writing a finishing chapter to the book, I needed to add about ten thousand words to bring the novel to the appropriate length. That took me aback—ten thousand additional words seemed like a major project. Up until now I had only written short stories. My major task had been to develop a clever opening and a surprise ending. That probably involved only a few thousand words. Filling in everything between the opening and closing was, to my mind, a bit of drudgery. I was not particularly adept at flowery descriptions or even diversions from a tight script that presented some philosophical discussion or tried to set a scene. I usually was intent on the story, not the setting. But I had a lot of words that were unused, and I just needed to get to it.

Looking at my aunt's draft to find areas that could be expanded, new thoughts or characters added, became my primary focus. I decided that one storyline that could be interesting was to develop the idea of an affair between the fellow who had been killed and John's wife. An affair had been going on for several years, but John had only recently found out about it. He killed Fred.

I decided that the plot was not tangled enough, too straightforward. It needed an interesting twist.

After several days thinking about how to write a surprise ending, I decided on the following: Leave the beginning of the story pretty much as Elsie had written it. John tells his wife he visited Fred when he did not. Fred is murdered. John is seen as the most likely murderer because of his admission to his wife and other testimony from someone who thought he was present at the scene of the crime. John's name is besmirched, he loses his clients, and his wife leaves him. Readers are left to believe that the "white lie" John told caused all this misfortune. But in the end John leaves town for a new life in the Bahamas, and readers discover that John did kill Fred, he knew about the affair between his wife and Fred, and he had taken a fair amount of money from one of his clients to support his new lifestyle.

I then had another thought about how to end the story. The basic plot is the same, with John telling the "white lie" but being innocent of killing Fred. Nevertheless, he is considered the prime suspect, but nothing can be proved. After his life is wrecked, his wife leaves him, and his business is in ruins, he runs away from Vero. He later uncovers some evidence that indicates his wife killed Fred. Trying to clear his name, he comes back to Vero and confronts his former wife. She confesses to killing Fred and pleads with him to not turn her into the police. She convinces him to take her back as his wife, but all the time she is plotting to kill him and make it look like a suicide. A bit convoluted, but it could work.

I went to bed thinking I finally had a plot that worked for Elsie's novel. At about three in the morning, I awoke with a new addition to the plot, one that I thought worked even better. I quickly got up, went to my desk, and opened the computer to write it down so I would not forget it in the morning.

In this version, Fred is married to Jane, who discovers he is fooling around with John's wife. She kills Fred with a long knife. She is not considered a suspect because she had been visiting friends in Denver for a couple of weeks prior to the death of her husband and was crafty enough to hide the fact that she had returned to kill her husband. Due to his white lie, John is the prime suspect for the murder, especially because Fred had been killed with a knife. John's wife had admitted that her husband was a sport fisherman and often used knifes to clean the fish he caught. John's law career is destroyed. His wife leaves him. To start over, he relocates to Bermuda. One day he gets a call from Fred's former wife Jane, who happens to be visiting Bermuda on vacation. She says she has always suspected he's innocent of her husband's death, and that she had always assumed that John's wife had killed her husband because John had wanted to end the affair. Jane and John agree to have lunch. Over lunch they become somewhat infatuated with one another. Dinners follow the luncheon. Jane moves in with John. A couple of years later, John is cleaning up the house—something that Jane rarely was inclined to do. After he washes her clothes, he begins putting her bras and panties in her bureau when at the bottom of the drawer he discovers a long knife. What to do now? He goes for a long walk on the beach trying to sort things out. His conclusion is: Jane is great at sex, better than his former wife. Fred deserved to be killed for cheating on his wife with John's wife. And he, John, could live happily ever after with Jane.

I got up in the morning and read what I had written the night before. As is often the case, these nighttime inspirations turn out a bit underwhelming when read the next day.

I would have to figure out what ending worked best. Regardless, I still had several thousand words to add before my agent would be satisfied. What had I gotten myself into?

CHAPTER TWENTY

TIME TO VISIT THE SPIRITUAL CAMP

I made reservations at the inn. I decided that two days would be sufficient. As I drove north, I thought about how I would approach investigating activities at the camp. I realized that there was little hard evidence of any wrongdoing and nothing that connected any of this to the deaths of my aunt or Alan. What was I going to do there other than nose around and get a feel for the place?

When I arrived at the check-in for the inn, it was clear they knew who I was and had suspicions about my intentions. The woman checking me in said she remembered my aunt's visit several weeks ago, referring to her as the "author." The reference to "my aunt" suggested that they had checked on me as well. I asked about getting appointments with mediums and was told that several of the mediums had left for the next few days and those that remained had full schedules. Clearly I was not going to get an appointment to have my fortune told or get any information from them.

One of the camp's staff visited me in my room and expressed regret over my aunt's death and indicated that they knew I was finishing her novel. They apparently had looked at my Facebook and website where that information had been posted. I told him that the book I was finishing had nothing to do with the camp. It was a novel totally unrelated to the camp.

I signed up for a bus tour of the camp. It was very interesting to hear the story of the town and have various houses pointed out and connected with the people who founded the camp. The town reminded me of a New England village. Small white houses, most of them made of wood, unremarkable except that a few had the same "door to nowhere" as my aunt's house. The doors were said to be a way that "spirits" could easily enter or leave the houses. The guide said that many of the homes were used only during the winter, a typical Florida situation. I wondered about what the spirits did during the summer season.

After wandering around the camp for a day, I decided that staying any longer was a waste of time and money. I had found out nothing of value, and if my aunt and Alan had been victims of some strange malicious spirits, I was only calling attention to myself. My visit may have been a dangerous mistake.

I decided to have dinner and drinks in the inn the last night at the camp. Sitting at a table in the dining room, I thought about this strange village. Deep in thought, I felt a hand on my shoulder. A bit startled, I found myself looking into the eyes of a rather unusual woman—red hair, strikingly beautiful in an odd way, and with a very seductive voice. I immediately thought of Abigale Cruz, the woman Alan Brooks described in his note about the strange ceremony he witnessed when he visited the camp.

She said, "I am sorry to bother you, Mr. McKenzie, but I wanted a moment of your time. I am Abigale Cruz."

"You are not bothering me; have a seat. I will get you a drink if you are interested in one."

"Thanks. I would like a scotch and water. The bartender knows what brand I drink. I wanted to talk with you about your aunt and your visit here."

I could not keep my eyes off her. She was mesmerizing, and as she began to talk about my aunt I found my attention wandering back to her. She recounted her first meeting with my aunt after she had taken the role as head of the camp. Apparently, my aunt was not pleased with her decision to bring in some new mediums that were aggressively trying to increase donations to the church and hype their séances using information collected on their clients. My aunt also was concerned that some of the new personnel brought into the camp were more interested in raising money than the spiritual health of the congregation.

Leaning toward me and perhaps accidentally brushing her knee with mine, Abigale said, "I assured Elsie that she was mistaken that I was more interested in making the camp and the church more profitable at the expense of the spiritual health of the congregation. I was promoted by the directors of our spiritual village because the camp and the church had been operating at a deficit for a number of years. I did tell Elsie if the séances had been helping make her books more profitable, as she had told the camp staff numerous times, that she might show her appreciation by helping support the camp financially."

Abigale then smiled at me and put her knee directly against my knee. "Your aunt, you know, Robert—may I call you Robert?—was a strong-willed woman who, once she made up her mind, was not inclined to change it. I assume her nephew is similarly inclined." She laughed, and I laughed as well. "I would like to get to know you better in hopes I can influence you to understand how dedicated I am to the spiritual well-being of all who come here seeking solace and"—she looked directly into my eyes—"love."

I was impressed by what she said and even more impressed by this beautiful and sexy woman. There is little question that I had fallen under her spell. If she had asked me to run away with her, I would have gladly gone. We spent the next hour or so in casual conversation, mostly her asking me about my life and my aunt. She did say how sorry she was about the accidents involving her and her friend Alan. She was particularly interested in whether or not I planned to finish her book on the camp. I told her that my immediate problem was to complete a mystery Elsie had begun but not finished. I said I did not know about whether I wanted to work on the other book, but I did want to continue her mystery series. Abigale pressed me on whether I would work on the book about the camp and said she was very concerned about anything that would raise concerns about the spiritual camp. I did commit to talking with her about anything I wrote about the camp. She seemed a bit relieved but not totally convinced.

She thanked me for spending time with her and said how much she enjoyed my company. She said that she thought she would be coming to Vero Beach the next week and suggested that the two of us get together for dinner. She also expressed particular interest in visiting my aunt's house because of its strong connection with the spiritual camp. Standing up, she bent over, kissed my cheek, and walked away, leaving my mind ablaze.

Driving back to Vero, I recovered my balance and tried to put all that I knew in some perspective. I would go back to my aunt's house and try to bring some order to my thoughts. I tried to put Abigale out of my mind but did so with some difficulty.

What did I "know"? What did I "suspect"? What, if anything, should I do about it? A pretty daunting set of questions.

I knew that both my aunt and Alan had fallen to their death in questionable circumstances. Both had been involved in an investigation of the spiritualist camp. The camp had some questionable tactics to raise money. But there was no direct evidence that the camp's activities were illegal even if they were open to question. Assuming the spirit world was responsible for the death of my aunt and her detective was crazy. I could not bring myself to believe in the spirit world, although I guess I did accept that there could be "good" spirits. Well, if there are good spirits, could there be evil spirits? I had one nagging thought—Abigale had mentioned the "accidents" involving my aunt and Alan. I had never mentioned Alan or his death. How did she know about Alan's accident?

Over the next week, Abigale was never totally out of my mind. I wanted to call her but thought that it was a bit too obvious. So, I waited and hoped for a call from her. I was acting like a teenager in love, waiting for a telephone to ring. It finally did, and I could hardly restrain myself from admitting that I had been waiting by the phone.

Abigale said she was coming to Vero on business the next week and wondered if I was available for dinner. "Available" was not the word I would have used. More like "panting." We made arrangements to meet at the Costa d'Este Beach Resort where she was staying, and I called for dinner reservations there. The hotel was within walking distance of my house—maybe I could lure her there. The next week was an anxious one for me. I was clearly infatuated with Abigale and could hardly wait to see her again.

On the designated night, I walked down Beach Drive from my house to the hotel, which was located on the ocean. I was dressed like a local with a bright sports shirt, blue blazer, and white pants. I should have worn a Jimmy Buffett straw hat but had decided that was a bit too much. Walking into the hotel and then the dining room, I looked around for Abigale. I was a bit early and asked to be seated, ordering a dirty martini. I looked around and began wondering if I had gotten the date or the time wrong.

Then I felt a tap on my shoulder, and there she was. She had a knack for sneaking up on a person. Dressed in a brightly colored, flowery outfit with a deep-cut neckline, she was ravishing. I pulled out a chair for her and tried to say something clever but only managed to mumble a greeting. I asked her about the trip down from the camp, and she indicated that it was an easy drive, although Highway 95 was busy as usual. We lapsed into the routine conversation about weather and subjects that I cannot recall. I ordered her a drink—Irish whiskey on the rocks—and asked for another dirty martini, this time with extra olives.

At some point in the conversation, she asked about my background.

CHAPTER TWENTY-ONE

BACKGROUNDS ARE EXPLORED

"You were a police detective, I believe. How did you get into that line of work?" Abigale asked.

"After a couple of years at Florida State, I decided to join the army where I became a military policeman. After leaving the army, I spent two years at Indian River College taking law enforcement courses. Then I answered an ad from the Denver police. After a few years on the force, I became a detective and served in that position until I was injured in an automobile accident. I was married for a couple of years, but my wife could not adjust to the irregular schedule of a detective. Missing dinner, appointments, and birthdays became too much, and we separated in a somewhat civilized way."

Abigale listened carefully and asked a few questions. As dinner progressed, I asked her how she got involved with the camp. At first, she was reluctant to talk about her past, but another scotch whiskey seemed to loosen her tongue a bit.

Apparently, her parents were very religious. Her parents quickly became aware that their daughter had some unusual talents. Even as a very young girl she could look into the future and read the thoughts of others. For several years it was just an amusing skill, but when she showed an interest in the occult, they became very worried because it was so contrary to their religious beliefs. They tried to persuade her not to engage in what they believed was magic. They even got her to go to a therapist hoping she might become more "normal." Her parents were killed in a house fire in Orlando. After their deaths, she went to England for a gap year and attended an unusual school called Arcanorium College.

"Arcanorium was a radical college," she said. "It offered workshops and discussion groups plus lectures given on subjects such as sorcery, divination, chaos, magic, and the history and the culture of magic. During Christmas vacation, my boyfriend, Clay Shepard, visited me. Unfortunately, he died in an accident in the London underground when people rushing to get on a car pushed him onto the tracks in front of an oncoming train. He died a few days before Christmas. I was going to go to London with him but needed to finish a paper that was due the next day. It was a tragic accident all the more so because we had just been talking about getting engaged." I expressed my condolences, but she barely noticed before continuing with her next adventure.

"I returned to the U. S. and spent the next year at the University of Florida completing my degree. I then chose to go to the Cherry Hill Seminary. Cherry Hill offered courses in ministry and pagan and nature-based spiritualities. After graduating from Cherry Hill, I applied for a vacancy as the assistant of ministry at the spiritual camp. The minister and I became very close and even considered getting married, but he died suddenly." She did not provide any details on the death of the minister although she mentioned his name, Ross McDonald, and said the death occurred in 2008.

"I was asked to fill the position. That is my story. I now am not only the minister at the camp but the director of the facility."

I thought about all she had told me about her past and could not resist asking, "How did you get involved in spiritualism and the occult?"

She sat for some time before answering, and then told me the following about her involvement in the spirit world:

"Early in life I knew that I had special powers. Even as a small child I had the ability to look into the future. Maybe it was just particularly sensitive attention to what was going on, what people said, how they acted, but I often could guess what was going to happen, what presents were going to be given to me, who would visit, and sometimes serious predictions like foreseeing accidents or the deaths of relatives who were ill.

"At first my parents were amused by my 'powers' and often showed them off to friends and relatives. Then they became a bit alarmed by my ability to predict and started to worry. My friends at school were fascinated by my ability to look into the future, but they also began to treat me a bit differently and keep their distance.

"I found that I was most comfortable among people who had experience with the occult. I read everything I could find about paganism, reincarnation, mystics, and communicating with spirits. I found a few like-minded people at university and joined some groups that discussed 'the other world.'

"Both my parents and siblings became very concerned when I began talking about attending a college in England that taught courses in the occult and paganism. They tried to talk me out of studying mysticism, suggested that I talk with a Catholic priest they knew, and even mentioned the idea of an exorcism."

I was impressed by her history but also a bit alarmed. There were too many deaths around her. My detective instincts told me that coincidences occurred, but as often as not there were more behind them than happenstance. My mind turned to subjects other than her history. I asked her if she was interested in sharing a bottle of Champagne in her room before we parted. She considered the suggestion but said she had an early appointment and needed to get some sleep.

She said, "Some other time. I won't forget."

Before we parted, we exchanged cards. Doing that made me feel a bit like a real estate broker. But at least I had some valuable information about Abigale. She hugged me, kissed me lightly on the lips, turned, and walked away quickly.

I walked home very disappointed but optimistic.

CHAPTER TWENTY-TWO

TRUDY

The next morning, I was sitting in the small patio at the back of my townhouse drinking a strong coffee.

"Robert, Robert." It was my neighbor Trudy calling over the wall separating our houses. "Robert, are you there? I thought I would bring over some sweet rolls." I knew what Trudy wanted. I had told her that I was going to dinner with a rather exotic woman. Trudy wanted a report on the dinner and on my "exotic friend." She came into the patio through the back gate, followed by her large female cat.

"Hello, Charles," I said. A strange name for a female cat but appropriate once you got to know Trudy better. Charles and I were well acquainted, and in fact I had a bowl of cat nibbles under the table on the patio. Trudy sat down at the table with an expectant look on her face. She waited patiently for a while but then said, "How did dinner with your new friend turn out?" I told her about the dinner and the stories Abigale told about what happened to some of her family and friends. Being connected with Abigale did not always turn out well. She'd mentioned several deaths of people she had been close to.

Without blinking an eye, Trudy asked, "Did she spend the night with you?"

"Boy you are nosey, but the answer is no; she had a long day and was looking forward to an even busier one."

Trudy seemed satisfied with the answer and asked, "What did you think of her after spending an evening together?"

"I am still fascinated with her. She is the most unique and interesting woman—other than you of course—that I have met. I can hardly wait to see her again. I think she is way out of my class, but nevertheless if she will see me again, I will jump at the chance."

It was clear that Trudy was not convinced that I was acting sensibly. She said, "Robert, be careful. This woman sounds like a handful, and I mean a handful of trouble." I did not disagree but was still attracted to Abigale. Trudy and I left our conversation about Abigale at that and moved on to other subjects. I was sure she would come up in the future.

* * *

That afternoon, my thoughts returned again to the previous evening and particularly to Abigale's history. My detective instincts clicked in, and I began to seriously address what Abigale had described in the review of her life. I found my notebook and wrote down the chronology of events connected to Abigale.

Born in Orlando	*1978*
U of Florida	*1996*
Death of family in Orlando	*1998*

Attended Arcanorium College England	*1999*
Death of college friend	*1999*
U of Florida	*2000-1*
Divinity School	*2003*
Asst Minister Spiritual Camp	*2004*
Death of Minister	*2008*
Death of Elsie	*2018*
Death of Alan	*2018*

When listed this way, the deaths seemed pretty startling. It would be interesting to look into each of them to provide some detail and also to look at where Abigale was during each death. At least the process would ease my mind that she was not involved. I decided that over the next week I would begin an investigation into each of the incidents she described. I would start with the death of her parents in a fire in their home in Orlando.

CHAPTER TWENTY-THREE

INVESTIGATION

Case Study One—The Cruz Family, Orlando, 1998

I decided to begin by looking at Orlando newspapers to see if I could get some information on the fire. I knew the year but not the precise date. Fortunately, the newspaper was digitized, and it was possible to find a report on the fire. Apparently, the fire was the result of a gas leak that led to an explosion at the house. Both Mr. and Mrs. Cruz died in the fire. The article indicated that they were survived by a daughter, Abigale Cruz, and a son, David Cruz. The article indicated Abigale was a student at the University of Florida, and David was married and lived in Orlando.

I decided to see if David was listed in the telephone book. There were several David Cruzes listed, but after six phone calls to David Cruz I was able to get in touch with Abigale's brother and arranged to meet him at his home. I concocted a story that I was writing an article that involved his sister and needed some background information on her. I found the house with little trouble after an easy drive from Vero to

Orlando. I found that the two had largely cut off relations, but David seemed willing to talk about his sister. We talked about the death of his parents and Abigale, and he raised a particularly interesting issue. He said his parents were very concerned about Abigale's interest in magic, the spirits, and paganism. They were sufficiently alarmed that they had contacted a Catholic priest who had conducted exorcisms. When they mentioned their concern and the idea of an exorcism to Abigale, she was absolutely outraged. In fact, that was when she announced she was spending a year in England at a school that had courses in magic and paganism. The fire occurred a week after this confrontation between their parents and Abigale. David and I had some further discussion about his sister, but the only new information was that the police had confirmed Abigale was in class when the fire started.

I had one more call to make regarding the fire and that was to the local fire marshal to see if I could get some additional information on the fire that killed the Cruzes. I did locate the fire marshal that had been involved in the investigation of the fire at the Cruz family's residence. He could not remember many details and did not have access to the report on the fire, but he did recall that it appeared that an accelerant, probably gasoline, had been spread around the foundation and ignited.

Case Study Two—Death of Clayton Shepard, Christmas, 1999

Any investigation of Shepard's death was going to be more complicated because it happened overseas. I began with the usual tactic of looking at newspaper reporting. It took a while because I only knew that Shepard died shortly before Christmas in a London underground. I looked at the *London Times* for the days between December 21 and 24, 1999. I found the story written on December 23, a Thursday—"Florida college student killed in freak accident." The story indicated that Clayton Shepard had fallen to his death in the Victoria Station as a crowd pushed forward waiting for an oncoming train. Mr. Shepard was visiting a friend in Bristol and apparently was in London looking at the sights. His death was considered by transit police to be an accident involving visitors inexperienced in using the underground.

I had few leads to follow, but suddenly I remembered a contact I had in Scotland Yard. Several years earlier, I had attended the FBI course offered to state and foreign police officers at the FBI Academy in Quantico, Virginia. At that course, I had met a senior police officer from Scotland Yard, or more correctly, the Metropolitan Police. I remembered his name: Archibald Simpson. We had become very friendly, and he'd given me his address and telephone number and said to call any time or even come to London to visit. I called and told him what I was about and asked if he could check any available records and see if there was anything out of the ordinary about Clayton Shepard's death. Archy said he would get back to me in a day or so, but he did not think he could turn up any information. But about a week later I got an email that provided some details on the police investigation into Clayton's death. A number of people on the platform at the time he fell were interviewed. Most had nothing significant to say, but one said he saw a person in a black raincoat and a woman with bright red hair standing very close to Clayton just before he fell onto the tracks. He mentioned that he thought the three of them were together because they were standing so close. There was nothing else in the email that shed any light on the incident.

The investigation into the various deaths around Abigale was becoming a somewhat exciting exercise.

Case Study Three—Death of Ross McDonald, Minister at Camp, 1999

I didn't remember if Abigale had mentioned the name of her fiancé and the minister at the camp who died in an accident in 1999. I was able to get the name, Ross McDonald, from my aunt's file that included some newsletters from the camp. There was a short biography of McDonald in the file. He had gone to the Liberty Divinity School and applied for the job as minister at the camp upon graduation. He was only three years older than Abigale. Apparently well-liked by his congregation, he had done some graduate work on spiritualist believers and the spirit world and fit in well with the followers at the camp.

Ross was an active hiker and joined a group for a trek along one of the many trails in the mountains of North Carolina. The group he was hiking with said that Ross was standing on the edge of a cliff when all of a sudden he threw up his arms and fell off the edge. The Park Service recovered his body, and they interviewed his companions. It was considered an unfortunate accident, and there was no further investigation.

AK

At this point I had investigated the deaths that Abigale mentioned. She was not implicated in any of them. I felt somewhat relieved, but as a detective I learned to be leery of abundant 'coincidences.' Often where there is smoke there is fire. But to finish the "case" properly and attempt to put my mind at rest, I needed to find out where Abigale was when my aunt and her detective died.

Case Study Four—Death of Elsie McKenzie, March 15, 2018

Elsie died late afternoon or early evening on March 15. The Ides of March was a date with sinister meaning. It was not difficult to search the camp website for their calendar. On the 15th of March, Abigale was leading the congregation in a spiritual celebration of the Ides of March with a program on the history of spiritualism and some type of service that went well into the evening. Probably dancing nude in a circle. At least she was not in Vero Beach.

Case Study Five—Death of Alan Brooks, July 8, 2018

Alan fell off the deck at the rest home sometime midday. I went back to the camp website and could only find one reference to Abigale during the week of July 8, a Thursday. But that one note indicated that she was busy that week with classes. Again, she was at the camp, not in Vero Beach.

I remembered other disturbing information that needed checking. Alan had mentioned that the bartender at the camp said that people who were writing negative things about the spiritualists had "bad experiences." I decided that I needed to open another case. Who were these people, and what were these "bad experiences"?

Case Study Six—Incidents Involving Critics of the Camp

This search was like looking for a needle in a haystack. The internet was my source, but as usual I had to wade through endless notices on how to lose weight, get a clear complexion, get potency back, or grow hair. But persistence paid off, and I found a couple of newspaper articles reporting accidents involving people who had been to the camp.

The first article was in a newspaper from Melbourne. It reported an accident that happened on a highway south of Melbourne in which two people were killed after their car went into a canal. The husband and wife were reporters from a local newspaper who had been on an assignment to write a story about the Spiritual and Health Camp. The couple spent only a few days at the camp and were on their way home when the accident occurred.

The couple had emailed a draft of their story to the newspaper before they left the camp. There was not a great deal of detail in the article, but it clearly expressed skepticism about many of the spiritualist practices they observed—palm reading, visions, and communication with the dead. They described the visitors at the camp other than those who were just curious as dupes being preyed upon by unscrupulous frauds.

According to the article, although the couple had checked in as singles, the camp staff quickly determined that they were together. They were given the cold shoulder, and it became apparent that someone had provided information that they were connected to the press. The couple apparently did not hide their feelings about spiritualism and were quickly ostracized.

The accident was described as unusual because it appeared that the car had driven straight into the canal without any skid marks and no evidence that another vehicle was involved. Autopsies showed that neither had been drinking, and there was no evidence that the driver suffered any kind of heart attack or stroke.

The second article I found involved an individual who had died of a heart attack at the camp. Again, it was in a local newspaper. Professor David Altmier had been doing research on spiritualism and spent several days at the camp talking to staff, attending various classes offered, and having his palm read and future told. He also had a session with one of the staff who claimed the ability to contact those who had passed on.

The article indicated that Professor Altmier had written several books and a variety of articles on spiritualism. He was both a believer and a critic of those suspected of fraud. Apparently, some of his writings argued that there are individuals who had the ability to not only look into the future but also to delve into the past and communicate with spirits.

It apparently was obvious the professor intended to be critical of the activities at the camp. He seemed to be in data collection mode but expressed some concerns about those communicating with the spirits during his sessions with camp personnel. He also asked a number of rather penetrating questions according to the camp staff.

There was no suspicion about the cause of the professor's death. A local coroner and camp doctor quickly determined that his death was caused by a fatal heart attack.

Chapter Twenty-Four

Dirt on the Camp

I needed to find out more about the camp. I intended to look through my aunt's files but decided it would be interesting to first look at local newspapers and the stories and see what the view of locals was toward the camp.

It took a while and some digging, but I finally found several newspapers in nearby towns that occasionally covered events at the camp. Many of the articles merely expressed skepticism about fortune telling and mystics and poked fun at those who went there to find out what the future held. There were a couple of articles that delved into the history of mysticism and its attraction.

For me the most interesting articles discussed several lawsuits that people had initiated against the camp. For example, one suit accused the camp of convincing an older lady to give her entire estate to the camp upon her death by promising they would keep her in touch with her dead husband. The article said that the family had initiated the suit claiming "mystics" had convinced their mother using fraudulent means that they could communicate directly with her dead relatives.

The suit was going to be reviewed by a judge. The article made the argument about why the case should be decided against the camp. But it also cited several other cases of this type when a court ruled that unless fraud could be proved, people had a right to give money to whomever they wished. There was no follow-up on exactly what happened in this case.

I found several other suits against the camp reported in various newspapers; it was not unusual for relatives to try and stop someone from giving money to the camp. My guess is that many of these disputes were settled out of court. Some money may have changed hands but perhaps the amount was negotiated. There was a piece in a Melbourne newspaper that caught my attention because it mentioned the name of a person suing the camp. Emily Jacobs was the niece of a woman who had intended to leave a considerable amount of money to the camp. She was also a lawyer. I found her name in the Melbourne directory and called. Surprisingly she answered the phone. When I told her I was doing some research on the camp with an emphasis on its money raising, she became particularly vocal.

Emily was not bashful about expressing her view. She said, "At first I thought that my aunt was getting her money's worth with some made-up conversations between her seer and her dead husband and son. My aunt was paying fifty dollars a session, and she was only having one session a month. But then she started talking about adding the camp and the church to her will. Finally, she reached the point where she intended to put the camp in her will, excluding most of her family from any inheritance."

It was at that point that Emily took the camp to court claiming undue influence on an older person, intimidation, and fraud. The judge supported some of the claim and appointed a third party to resolve the issue. The will was rewritten with a smaller amount going to the camp.

Emily said, "My aunt never fully forgave my interference."

One thing I did see in other articles written about the camp and particularly the church was a strong feeling that the entire enterprise was somehow anti-Christian with overtones of the Devil. This feeling seemed to run very deep and was more concerning to locals than the involvement of seers and fortune tellers.

The camp newsletters had no mention of the lawsuits or the surrounding community's concerns about the camp.

I can't say I was relieved after my investigation was over. But I felt better having looked at each incident and traced where Abigale was at the time each occurred. Something was not right, but I could not figure out what had happened to explain or connect the various incidents in her life. I decided that maybe it was not possible to "explain" what had happened. Abigale was unusual, her life was unusual, and events surrounding her were unusual. Maybe that was enough to know.

I could not resist telling my neighbor Trudy about my investigation. I went through it with her case by case. When approached this way it seemed like the outline of a murder mystery. I took pains to say that these incidents happened over a ten-year period and there was no reason to believe that they were connected. In fact, I paid specific attention to where Abigale was during these "accidents."

Trudy was not convinced. She said, “The connection is Abigale, plain and simple. You are so besotted by her you cannot see the obvious. You need to get away from her as quickly as possible or you will become one of her victims. She truly is an evil force!”

I could not accept that judgment about Abigale. Just couldn’t. I needed to see her, and several more times I drovc up to the camp and had dinner with her.

CHAPTER TWENTY-FIVE

SPACE ALIENS

I had become somewhat friendly with Ben the bartender at the camp's inn. Usually when I came to take Abigale to dinner I would arrive early, as is my bent, and she would not be ready to leave for an hour or so later. She was that busy and that conscientious about her work. I would sit at the bar and nurse a drink and talk to Ben.

I quickly discovered that Ben was not really into spiritualism. It was his wife, Alice, who like Abigale got involved in "the other side" early on. Since few people sat at the bar early in the evening, Ben proved to be lonely, talkative, and a bright guy.

"Is spiritualism a religion?" I asked.

In a somewhat hushed voice and leaning toward me, Ben said, "I wouldn't call it that. From what I can figure out, there are two types of people who come to the camp. Those who believe that the descendants of a lot of former outer space aliens are here on Earth among us. The second type are those who focus more on reincarnation. Perhaps both are right."

I had never before heard of our planet being infested with former outer space aliens. "The outer space alien believers contend that there are twelve planets in our universe," Ben said by way of explanation. "Hitler believed this, too, my wife told me. Those who are indigenous to the outer planets of the sun tend to be more detached, rational. Those whose original ancestors came from planets closer to the sun are more emotional. God permitted us to gather together here on Earth so we can learn to be more God-like and learn to get along. I am not making this up. My wife says they believed there was harmony when each of the twelve races lived on their respective planets. The problem is the Aryans, the ones Hitler championed, tend to be totally rational and outthink the rest of us and ended up being in charge. Western civilization is dominated by alien descendants of the outer planets. Twelve is the significant number. There are twelve signs of the Zodiac. Twelve tribes of Israel. Christ had twelve apostles."

I gave a look at Ben's Nordic face, blue-eyed, straight nose, and blonde hair. "I assume your ancestors came from the outer planets."

He laughed. "You Irish mutts are all screwed up, according to my wife, because when the Spanish Armada was sunk off the shores of England in the 1600s, a lot of closer planet descendants copulated with your blue-eyed cold-blooded relatives."

"I'm mostly Scottish," I said. "Same church, different pew," Ben responded.

Ben gave more credence to those reincarnation spiritualists who believed that they had inhabited Earth a number of times. "My wife, Alice, tells me she has been reincarnated ten times. Alice said Earth is a training place, allowing you to get better and better or sometimes get worse, and then you have to come back to get better. Look, at first I thought Alice was a bit off her rocker. But I soon found her premonitions right on. And once, early on in our marriage when a woman I knew at my job was coming on to me and I was thinking about cheating on Alice, Alice woke up one night screaming, and when I asked what was wrong, she slapped me hard on my face. 'What's that for?', I yelled. She then told me she had a dream that I was thinking of fooling around with a woman at work, and she described the woman to a tee. Alice says I've only been reincarnated four times, and that's why I can't really comprehend old souls like her. She and I were sisters together in another lifetime, she contends. People are reincarnated together often to learn to handle the difficult negative interactions they had in their earlier incarnations. It seems I cheated with her husband the last time we were together, and that's why I have to support her in this incarnation. She, being an old soul, did not have to come back. She did it so I could evolve into a higher spiritual soul."

Abigale showed up as Ben and I were talking, and Ben immediately changed the subject, asking about a player who I had never heard of on the Baltimore Ravens football team. Abigale was suspicious. I could tell by the look she gave Bill. In the car, she began questioning me about what Ben and I were talking about. I told her that he and I both liked football. I suspected she did not believe me, but she dropped the inquiry.

The next time I sat at the bar nursing a beer as I waited for Abigale, I was aware that Ben was a lot more circumspect in talking to me about what takes place at the spiritual camp. But I kept pressing him.

"What kind of people come here to attend the séances and psychic readings?" I asked. He looked around, perhaps to see if Abigale was approaching, and said, "All kinds, but mostly older women, some foreigners as well. You know I have to be careful about talking about what goes on here."

"Foreigners?" I asked.

"A few somewhat upper crust types who I'm told work for the United Nations," he said. "Alice said it doesn't surprise her. When she was in New York City, she used to go to the United Nations Plaza, a big building next to the UN. She said the second or third floor has one of the largest collections of occult and metaphysical libraries in world."

I probably looked like I did not believe what he was saying. "Look, this camp and Abigale are a pretty big thing among believers in this stuff. Other spiritualists hold Abigale in high regard. They also seem to be afraid of her." Ben looked around again to see if Abigale was nearby. "Alice said Abigale can put a hex on those who cross her, and the spirits can cause them grief. The spirits can mess with their minds."

"I thought this camp was to help people get closer to God," I said.

"Not the God you and I grew up learning about," Ben replied. He then spotted Abigale and thanked me loudly for the five-dollar tip I never gave him and walked to the other side of the bar.

"Ben telling you more secrets," Abigale said in a voice loud enough for Ben to hear.

"He told me the Broncos won't win their division, and I should not bet on the San Francisco Forty Niners either."

As we walked out of the inn, Abigale turned her head and gave Ben a harsh look.

The next time I came early to take Abigale out to dinner, Ben was nowhere in sight. A woman was tending the bar. As I ordered my beer, I inquired about Ben. "He's no longer here," she said and moved away from me to wash some glasses.

Later at dinner, I asked Abigale about Ben. "We had to let Alice, his wife, go. It was very sad. Alice and I worked together before she married Ben. I think she returned to Manhattan, where she grew up. Apparently, she and Ben were not getting along. They might be getting a divorce. Ben's back there trying to patch things up. I don't think he'll return."

Early the next week, I got another call from Abigale. She said she was very busy at the camp and would not be able to come down to Vero for some time. She suggested that we keep in touch using the internet and messaging. She seemed very excited about being in regular communication with me, indicating that she really enjoyed talking to me at dinner and exchanging views and learning about each other. I remembered the long conversation we had about our experiences, travel, and even books that we had recently read.

She did say that she still wanted to come to Vero to see my aunt's house and then go to dinner. Despite my concerns about her complicated history, I was looking forward to seeing her but was anxious to stay in touch via the internet. I was unsure of my long-term intentions, but I did clean up my house and put clean sheets on the bed. You never know.

CHAPTER TWENTY-SIX

MY EX CALLS

One evening I decided to look at my telephone messages, something I had ignored for several days. Going through them, I saw that my ex-wife, Susan, had called and left a message: "Robert, give me a call. We have not been in contact for some time, and I am worried about you. You have my number. Call as soon as you can." I was a bit puzzled. We had not been in touch for perhaps a year or so when she had then called and updated me on what was going on in her life. At that time, she had spelled out in some detail what had happened to her and what she was doing. More than I wanted to know. She said that her second marriage had gone onto the rocks, and she was living by herself. Our breakup had been fairly civil, although to paraphrase the country music song, "She got the gold, and I got the shaft." At least that is what it seemed like at the time when she got the house and some of my salary. But that was years ago, and I did not hold a grudge. I sat there for some time thinking about whether or not I wanted to call Susan back. We had a good marriage, but she just could not adjust to the hours of a police detective and decided she needed a more stable household. I was worried about what she wanted from me. My life was fully occupied by another woman—Abigale. That was challenging enough, and I did not need a further complication.

A couple of days later, I decided I needed to return Susan's call. Our conversation started with the usual polite "sorry I did not call sooner" and "how are you doing" exchanges. It was not long, however, before Susan got to the point of her earlier call. She said, "I had this dream about you. You were in a great deal of trouble and needed help. It involved a woman who you were totally infatuated with to the point where you could think of nothing else. That woman had a strange hold on you."

I replied, "I am totally involved with a woman who is, to say the least, unusual and very interesting. She is not evil. I do not need help and am not in trouble. But I thank you for calling and for your concern." Susan mumbled something that I could not understand and then changed the subject to what I had suspected was the reason for her call in the first place. She said, "I want to talk with you about renewing our relationship. My second marriage was a failure, and one of the reasons was that I kept comparing my new husband to you, and he always came out second. I know this may come as somewhat of a shock, but I never wanted to separate from you. We had such a good time, and then I became frustrated because you were spending so much time at work and neglecting me. I don't want you to answer now, but think about the idea of our getting together again."

I was not too surprised by Susan's comments. I certainly was not going to jump at her idea. We did have a good life, but a number of years had passed, and I was a different person now. Besides, I thought I had found a true and passionate love—Abigale. I decided that it would be unwise to let Susan believe there was a chance that we could get together again. I did say, "I appreciate your thoughts about our past and agree that it was generally a happy relationship, but I do not see much hope for renewing our relationship. Too much water has passed under the bridge, and I expect both of us have changed." Susan was very reluctant to end the conversation, saying, "You never know what might bring us together again. I think the common interests we shared might more than compensate for the changes each of us have undergone over the last few years. We could make it work. At least think about our getting together again."

I sat for some time after Susan hung up, thinking about our life together and the good times we had. But then I reviewed my life at this moment and decided that I did not want to go back—only ahead. My attraction to Abigale remained, and all I could think about was getting an email from her. I was not going to give her up.

CHAPTER TWENTY-SEVEN

EMAILS

Early the next week, I received my first email from Abigale. I will record the messages I received from her and the comments I made on each.

From: Spiritabigale@aol.com
To: Verorobert@aol.com

Robert:

I am so looking forward to getting to know you better, even if it is by way of the internet.

Although I am a pretty confident person, I find that sometimes I am a bit reluctant to share feelings in person. I am better with words written down than conversation.

I really enjoyed our discussion at the restaurant the other night. Your interest in my past and obvious sympathetic reaction to my problematic history was reassuring. I told you things that I have not mentioned to others.

Sharing confidences is something that I have done very cautiously in the past.

Look forward to your response and our future exchanges.

Love, Abigale

I found the message from Abigale both exciting and a bit surprising. I was warmed by the kind words about our earlier meeting and yet a bit concerned about the undertone of her message. She seemed a troubled person.

Here was my response:

To: Spiritabigale@aol.com
From: Verorobert@aol.com

Abigale:

Thanks for the note. You are very generous but correct in describing the conversation we had at dinner. It was refreshing to talk with you and find out something of your life. You certainly have had some interesting and troublesome events in your life but seem to have come out a stronger person.

Like you, I find talking in person rather more difficult than writing. It becomes even more difficult when I talk with you because you seem so self-confident and beautiful. A bit out of my class and reach.

Keep in touch.

Yours, Robert

To: Verorobert@aol.com
From: Spiritabigale@aol.com

Dear Robert:

I have really enjoyed our exchanges. Over my life I have had few men friends. My college lover was just that, and the relationship was physical. We seldom had discussions about anything but when we were going to go to bed next. My friendship with the minister at the camp was just that. He was more interested in my unique ability as a mystic than anything else. Before he died, I was beginning to think that he might be gay.

You are so easy to talk with, and I feel that there is nothing that I cannot tell you. That is such a relief because everyone at the camp wants something from me, and I am always on the alert to make sure I don't say or do something that is not consistent with my role as minister and camp administrator.

Love, Abigale

My exchanges with Abigale were beginning to feel a bit uncomfortable. What did she want from me? Was I willing to get this close to anyone, let alone this unusual woman? I was not sure she wasn't way out of my class, although I still wanted her.

CHAPTER TWENTY-EIGHT

THE CRUISE TO HELL

I had not heard from Abigale, by telephone or email, for over a week. I was beginning to wonder if I had said something wrong, if she was irritated at me, or if she was just busy. In any case, the email caught me by surprise. The content was even more surprising.

From: Spiritabigale@aol.com
To: Verorobert@aol.com

Dear Robert:

Sorry not to be in touch for a while. I have been busy at the camp and totally preoccupied with personnel actions. We have replaced some people on our staff and added some new people. That always adds to the problems and tensions of management. But that is not the reason I am writing you. I have received a proposal from a company that runs cruise ships out of Cape Canaveral. They want me to be the "host" of a three-day cruise in the islands. I would be billed as a spiritualist who will tell fortunes and hold séances for the passengers. I think it sounds like fun and besides, it offers a free cruise and hefty stipend.

What is more, I can bring a guest and will have a full stateroom. You will be my guest for a few days of cruising. We will have a great time.

Love, Abigale

It did not take more than a few minutes for me to make up my mind and accept her offer. Three days of sex with Abigale, on a cruise in the islands, with great food and drink. What more could I ask for? I sent her this response:

From: Verorobert@aol.com
To: Spiritabigale@aol.com

Sounds like a wish come true. A few days with you in my arms. Too much!

Love, Robert

A couple of days later, Abigale sent me some information on the cruise. The Queen of the Sea sailing out of Port Canaveral. A three-night cruise to the Bahamas and Nassau. She was arranging for a car to pick us up and deliver us to the port early in the morning. The ship departed between seven and eight and returned to the port three days later at seven in the morning. A car would meet us on our return. It sounded like she had everything under control.

The car arrived at my house very early in the morning. The driver said that Abigale had decided to spend the night at a motel close to the port and would meet me on the ship. That sounded like a wise decision; I wished I had done the same. Arriving where the Mariner was berthed, I dropped off my luggage and went aboard. I was told how to get to my cabin but decided to wander about the ship looking for Abigale. It was a beautiful ship, and although I had been on other cruises, I was impressed by its size and luxury.

I finally found Abigale surrounded by several people and talking to a very impressive, uniformed man. Listening to the conversation, I decided he was responsible for the entertainment and events on the ship. Abigale was telling him what she needed for her events and what she proposed to do. He listened carefully and took some notes. She clearly was getting what she wanted. She looked around and saw me and rushed over putting her arms around me. As she introduced me to the ship's officer and several other people standing there, it sounded like I was her "boy toy" along for the trip with no responsibilities other than to keep her amused.

We went off to our stateroom, but as soon as we got there, she had to rush off to begin her job entertaining those who had paid for the cruise. Her first tasks were to set up appointments for readings, schedule some séances, and arrange for her talks in the evening. She was going to be busy much of the day and early evening. It was clear that she expected me to attend most of her "performances," offering moral support.

She was interesting to watch in action. As people came to set up times for readings, she spent considerable time with each of them, asking questions and chatting. I then saw her write notes in a steno pad. She also spent some time at the ship's computer, and again she wrote some notes. It was not too hard to figure out what she was doing, learning something about each of the people that signed up for a reading. I found it interesting to watch her move around the room collecting information and getting her performance in hand. She did not have any readings or séances on the first day of the cruise; it was a preparation day. She continued the information collection activities during lunch and particularly at dinner. We had dinner with a large group of people, many of them the same people who had signed up for sessions with Abigale. She kept up a steady conversation with an emphasis on the background of each person, where they lived, their family, their interests. She was very good at eliciting information without seeming to pry but letting each person talk spontaneously. Abigale was good at this.

She was also very good in bed that first night, although I found she wanted to be the boss even in bed. I had nothing to complain about, but I was getting the feeling that I was a "kept" man.

The second day of the cruise was a whirlwind because Abigale was very busy with readings off and on throughout the day, and she conducted a séance for over a dozen people in the evening. I followed her around per instruction and sat close enough to hear the conversation during readings. Often Abigale merely confirmed what someone told her, adding a thought or an opinion, leading a bit but letting the "client" come to the appropriate conclusion. It was masterful. When finished, most of the people thought some new information had been received from Abigale but in fact they had been led to see their own thoughts with greater clarity.

The séance on the second night was pretty intense. Abigale had selected a woman in her mid-forties as the principal subject. This woman had lost her husband and son in a recent auto accident and was in great distress. She had been brought on the cruise by her parents, who hoped to take her mind off the recent tragedy. Abigale went into a trance-like state and tried to contact the husband, without success. Contact was made with the sixteen-year-old son, who indicated that he and his father were free spirits who were able to watch over their mother. He told his mother, through Abigale, that the three of them would be reunited and that he wanted her to get on with her life in the meantime. This seemed to offer some solace to the mother, and the session ended on a positive note.

After dinner, a dance band played some great '40s tunes. I asked Abigale to dance, but she said she was too tired after her full day. One of the ladies at our table came around to me and wanted to dance. Once on the floor, I realized what a good-looking woman she was and what a good partner. We danced together for much of the evening, and at some point, Abigale left for our cabin without my noticing. I got an earful when I went down. She was not happy about being ignored and made it clear that she had invited me on this cruise, and I was in her debt.

I don't need to add that the evening did not end on a positive romantic note.

Day three pretty much followed the pattern of the previous day. There were readings during most of the afternoon, and I noticed that Abigale was getting a bit short with some of her clients. Her patience was getting thin, and she ended some conversations a bit quickly. She was very rude to my dancing partner, who had become overly friendly with me.

The séance held the last night of the cruise was a disaster. Abigale had decided to focus on an elderly woman who seemed genuinely interested in contacting a dead brother. Just as Abigale said she was starting to get in touch with his spirit, the woman jumped to her feet and said this was all a gigantic fraud. She denied having a dead brother and called Abigale a hoax and the séance the previous night a damnable trick played on a vulnerable young woman. The séance ended abruptly, Abigale made some defensive remarks, but the audience began to break up. To make matters worse, I was sitting next to my dance partner from the previous evening. Once again Abigale stormed off. I went to the bar with my friend and had a nightcap. Probably a bad decision. Abigale was sleeping when I got to the cabin.

The ship arrived back at port early in the morning. Abigale and I had packed up with hardly a word to each other. We picked up some coffee and rolls at the cafeteria. A couple at the table said that they just heard that my dancing partner had fallen down the companionway last night and broken an ankle. I heard Abigale say under her breath, "It serves her right."

We found our transportation with hardly a word to each other. Abigale was first dropped off, and then I went home. What a voyage!

I realize that I have not said anything about the trip on the Mariner. I should have mentioned that I have been on cruises to the islands before. I was not impressed with the islands, although I enjoyed being at sea. The towns visited by cruise ships are small and dirty with little to see and only junk to buy. That is probably being a bit too harsh, but it is true. From a few hundred yards offshore, the islands look exotic. On shore they are not much, although a few have great beaches. On this trip, most of the time I was with Abigale, and between performances I either went on deck to look at the ocean or to the bar for an Irish whiskey or rum and soda. I enjoyed talking to the fellow passengers because they tend to be a diverse group.

Abigale seemed to resent any time I spent with others, so I was very careful except when she was fully engaged with her jobs.

All in all, it was not a "voyage from hell," but it certainly was not what I would call a good trip. I found out that Abigale could be pretty spiteful, and although she could be a great lover, that seemed to be something she could turn on or off at will. Ours was not an easy relationship. It took a lot of work, and at times I felt I was walking on eggshells. At the time I didn't know what to expect for our future, but looking back on it, there were certainly warning signs.

CHAPTER TWENTY-NINE

MORE EMAILS

To: Spiritabigale@aol.com
From: Verorobert@aol.com

Sweet Abigale:

Your notes are remarkably frank and revealing. I hope you don't expect too much from me. I am an ordinary person with the usual drives. Having intimate conversations even by mail with a woman as beautiful and dramatic as you seem is exciting but also a bit intimidating.

Perhaps we can get together again in Vero sometime soon.

Robert

To: Verorobert@aol.com
From: Spiritabigale@aol.com

Dear Robert:

I sense in your last note concern about getting too close. I do not want to scare you off. I am just excited about finding it so easy to talk and think about you.

I am looking forward to the time when we can sit across from one another, hold hands, and whisper sweet nothings. I know that I can be a bit intimidating but will try very hard to be your "friend" and more.

As you can tell, I am beginning to fall for you!

Love and Kisses, Abigale

PS: I think of you often and can barely wait for your emails.

The emails back and forth continued and became more intimate. I relaxed and decided that our relationship could last and grow into something permanent.

Early one evening I got a call from Abigale, who seemed distraught to say the least. She said that in her last email she had a note at the end declaring her love for me. But when she later looked at the "sent" mail, that comment had been deleted.

Abigale went on to say that she had talked to "them" indicating that "they" should stay out of her relationship with me, not interfere, and certainly not take any action against me. She was very upset and angry.

A bit confused, I asked, "Who is 'them' and 'they'?"

She calmed down a bit and said that she regularly communicated with "spirits" who advised her. They suggested courses of action, recommended she avoid certain things or people, and generally supported her.

That explanation did not reassure me. To the contrary, I began to wonder about my involvement with this strange lady. I decided that an email cooling down our relationship was in order. So, I sent this message:

To: Spiritabigale@aol.com
From: Verorobert@aol.com

Dear Abigale:

Your call was a bit upsetting. I just cannot fully comprehend this communicating with "spirits" or as you described them, "them" and "they." It is just more than I can understand or accept.

I do not know what to do. I am very fond of you but cannot imagine a relationship with someone who has direct involvement with the spirit world. Maybe the two of us should just back off a bit and see what happens.

Distraught, Robert

From: Spiritabigale@aol.com
To: Verorobert@aol.com

Dear Robert:

I know that some events in my life that I mentioned during our dinner together in Vero have worried you. You said that given your background as a detective the deaths of my family and two close friends seemed like more than just coincidence. You probably conducted your own investigation into these incidents. I decided to give you my side of the story about each of these events.

First, I need to say that I am disappointed that you did not directly ask me about the circumstances surrounding the deaths.

My mother and father did die in a fire at their home. It happened when I was at university. The fire started in the basement near the heating furnace. According to the fire marshal, one of the pipes bringing gas to the furnace was loose and the starting spark ignited the escaped gas. The entire house exploded in flame, killing my mother and father before any help was possible.

I do not know precisely what happened, but I have a possible explanation. My father thought of himself as a handyman capable of fixing anything. He was anything but handy and for years had turned simple repair jobs into major disasters. My mother had mentioned to me in a telephone conversation just before the accident that he was working on the furnace. Playing around with the gas connections was just the sort of thing he would do.

I believe that it is likely that my father did something that caused the gas leak. It was, plain and simple, an accident.

I will send another note on the other "accidents." Right now, I am tired and need to stop.

Love, Abigale

From: Spiritabigale@aol.com
To: Verorobert@aol.com

I am sending this explanation of my past in several emails because otherwise they can get a bit long.

The death of my college friend and lover, Clayton, at the Victoria underground station was a shock. The two of us had a great deal of fun together; he was my first real love. I was not with him when he fell in front of the train and do not know any more about the incident than what I was told by the Metro police.

Clayton had decided to spend the day in London. I had classes and could not go with him. I do know that before he left for the city and a day of touring, he had smoked several joints of marijuana and was feeling no pain. My assumption is that while standing on the platform waiting for an underground train, he lost his balance and fell in front of the train.

Love, Abigale

From: Spiritabigale@aol.com
To: Verorobert@aol.com

This is the last of three emails.

There is even less to say about the death of Ross McDonald. Although we were friends, and I worked closely with him as his deputy minister at the camp, we were not really soul mates. He was interested in me primarily because I had some unique powers including look into the future and communicating with spirits. These were powers that Ross was very interested in but did not have.

Again, I have no firsthand knowledge of Ross's death. Members of the group he was hiking with said that he was standing close to the edge of a cliff, lost his balance, and fell to his death. Ross tended to be a show-off, and whenever he had the chance, he would demonstrate how brave he was by some risky move.

That is all I know about the three deaths I mentioned at dinner. I think you also included your aunt and her detective friend in the list of unusual deaths. I know nothing about these last two and can only faintly remember talking with your aunt. I hope I have put your mind to rest.

Maybe we can restart our relationship with all this behind us. Don't worry about my unique powers—they are insignificant compared to the power you exert over me. You are my touchstone and communicating with you is more important than my communicating with spirits.

Love, Abigale

To: Verorobert@aol.com
From: Spiritabigale@aol.com

Dear Robert:

To really begin to understand who I am and what we attempt to achieve at our spiritual camp, I would like for you to attend one of our séances. I recommend your meeting Pamela Greer, a very clairvoyant seer and channel, and then attend a gathering (that's what we call it) in which she contacts the other side—the spiritual guides who facilitate seekers in communication with their loved ones who have passed to the other side. If you like, I would be happy to join you in the séance, and then we can have dinner after.

Love Abigale

CHAPTER THIRTY

THE SÉANCE

I actually was a bit frightened when I received this email from Abigale. Being a former detective, my entire professional background was rooted in the facts—"Nothing but the facts ma'am," as Joe Friday used to say on the television show *Dragnet*. Facts are things you can see, touch, feel, and exist in this world—not on the "other side."

But I also was drawn to Abigale in a weird way—yes, attracted to her physically, but more than that. She was a mystery to me. My detective nature needed to understand her not just as a person but someone who might be responsible in some way for my aunt's unusual accident.

I also was confused. I had never attended a séance, and I did not know what a seer was or what a clairvoyant seer was. Then this Pamela Greer was a channel as well. What the heck was a channel? Who were the spiritual guides from the other side? I was frightened and confused but intrigued. I finally decided intrigued had me. I agreed in a responding email to attend the séance but only if Abigale sat next to me to protect me.

The séance was to be held in the spiritualist's church at 5 p.m. I arrived at 4:30 p.m., early as is my habit. A striking raven-haired woman about the same age as Abigale was arranging chairs in a circle. There was something peculiar about her. I introduced myself. "You must be Abigale's friend," she said, without shaking my hand.

She must have noticed I was somewhat put off by her not shaking my hand. "I'm Pamela Greer," she said. "Sorry not to take your hand, but if I touch you, I start getting insights into you. Insights you probably don't want me to have. Abigale said this is your first time attending a séance," she said while continuing to place chairs in an increasingly larger circle.

I said yes and began helping her. "I'm a virgin," I said with a laugh. Just as I said this, Abigale walked in with a large group of people, mostly women who looked to be over sixty.

"I heard that!" she shouted. Abigale came over, hugged me, and then somewhat dramatically kissed me with her open mouth on the lips, the first time she had ever done that. "No virgin anymore."

Pamela moved away from Abigale and me, greeted all the people, about twenty or so, and instructed them to join her by sitting in the circle. It then dawned on me what was peculiar about Pamela. She was a witch. I said that to myself and could not believe that I thought that, because I do not believe in witches. The raven hair, fair skin, deep-set piercing blue eyes, high cheekbones, and attractive but pointed chin. Definitely a witch.

The lights were turned down in the church, and Pamela instructed us to be quiet and meditate on what we wanted the other side to say to each of us. "I am not in charge of this séance," she said. "The spiritual guides on the other side are. I don't know if your loved ones on the other side will speak to you or speak to your needs. All of us just need to be available. Sometimes nothing happens. But I have a strong feeling that this will be a very interesting time."

We all sat silent for at least twenty minutes. Abigale was next to me, and her leg was warm against mine, which made it difficult for me to concentrate on meditating. Finally, Pamela, who appeared to be in a deep trance, began to speak. But the voice that came out of her was that of a man. The voice was deep and resonated.

"I am Jo-el," the voice said. "I rarely have the honor to speak through Pamela Greer. Pamela has been among us many times prior to stepping down into her present incarnation. She is a very old and blessed soul. We are also honored that Abigale is among you here tonight. Another blessed old soul who I even shared a life with hundreds and hundreds of years ago as brother and sister. I was the sister, and she was my brother. Many of you will be blessed to communicate with a loved one. But what they may have to say to you is of their choosing, not mine. Also, we here on the other side are aware that some of you, and one in particular, are somewhat skeptical of what is now taking place." Abigale leaned her warm leg firmly against mine. "All I can say is listen with an open mind. Ours is not to coerce or convince. Ours is only to be a blessing."

Jo-el, speaking through Pamela, then asked if there was a Doris in the gathering. Two women said yes. "Doris K," Jo-el said.

"I'm Doris Kennedy," a large woman to the right of me said. Jo-el then spoke. "Your bother says your husband still needs some schooling on our side before he can communicate with you."

Doris said, "Some whipping might help." Everyone laughed.

Jo-el was not at all happy with what Doris said. "All of us," he said in a stern voice, "need instruction. It took me many years before I stopped abusing others."

Jo-el then called out for Marilyn.

"I'm here."

"Your young son who died before he was supposed to is here and says he misses you rubbing his head at night." Marilyn began weeping. "There, there Marilyn. He loves you too."

Jo-el continued mentioning names, and women, primarily, responded. Joe-el then asked if there were any questions from anyone. A man with close-cropped hair who identified himself as Harry spoke up. "I have a job offer in Minnesota. It's a great opportunity, I think, but it means uprooting my family. What should I do?"

Jo-el responded, "It is not for us on this side to make choices for you. That is why you are in your present incarnation. I can tell you that your son, who is not doing well in school here, will probably do better in Minnesota."

A younger woman wearing shorts then asked Jo-el, "I recently sold my rental property. Where do you think I should invest the money—in another property?"

Jo-el was quiet for a few moments. "I'm told," Jo-el said, "that property values in your area of the country will probably decrease over the next couple of years. You might want to wait awhile and then buy another rental."

I could not help myself. I asked, "My aunt recently had a fatal accident. Was it an accident?"

Jo-el was quiet for a moment or two before he said, "Elsie McKenzie is here and is aware of your concerns. All she will say is that she hopes you will finish the novel she was writing. She emphasized the word novel." Jo-el paused for a second and then continued and said, "Your mother is here with us. She wants me to tell you she is sorry she left you so suddenly. She should have never left you like that. She is crying."

I was shocked. Few people knew my mother had taken her own life. I thought back. I don't think the newspapers back then reported it as a suicide. In checking my background, if Abigale had someone do that, there wasn't any information that would have let Jo-el know that about my mother. The reason I was so close to my Aunt Elsie is that after my mother died, Elsie helped raise me. I had not even thought about my mother's death for the last twenty or so years.

Others then began asking questions. For some there was no one on the other side willing to speak. Most of the questions were about how their loved ones were coping on the other side. Finally, Pamela, as if coming out of a deep sleep, shook her head several times and spoke in her normal voice. "That's all. Sessions like this are very draining. I am not really aware of what was said, but it went so long I assume most of you are satisfied?" There was a spontaneous burst of applause. Someone turned on the lights. Abigale then took my hand and said, "Your treat for dinner?"

We took separate cars and met at Ocean Grill for dinner, a high-end restaurant that overlooks the Atlantic Ocean. After gin martinis at the bar, we moved to the dining area. Abigale ordered duck, and I a porterhouse steak, medium rare. Each time I started to discuss the séance, Abigale demurred. "Let's enjoy the meal and the view and just enjoy each other's company. We haven't been able to do that. After dinner, I'll drive over to your place for a night cap, and we can discuss what took place at our church, okay?" You think I was about to turn down that offer? No way.

After dinner we took our separate cars to my townhouse. We actually walked up to the door holding hands. As I brought out two glasses of Remy Martin XO cognac—I save it only for special occasions—she leaned back on my ten-year-old leather couch and slowly unbuttoned her blouse a bit, showing her breasts snuggling out of her black bra. "Okay, Mr. Detective, what did you think of the séance?"

Sitting down next to her, I took a sip of the cognac and decided not to look at her breasts. "Was there a lot of research by the church beforehand on all those who attended the séance?"

Abigale moved closer to me, put her leg over mine. "Not very trusting, are you? No, no research. The other side can read our minds to a degree. Not totally."

"What's with the voice that came out of Pamela?" I asked, moving closer to Abigale.

"Pamela is a channel. Only the highly evolved spiritualists can be channels. The spiritual guides speak through them. Most seers just hear those who speak from the other side, and sometimes they misinterpret what they hear. A channel has a direct line to the spiritual guide. Jo-el is very high up in the hierarchy. As he said, he and I grew up in the same family in Egypt nearly three thousand years ago."

Abigale instantly saw my disbelief. "I know this sounds very weird to you. But when I was very young, I too was a clairvoyant. I could see things before they happened. I could read other people's thoughts. It seemed so natural to me. My family thought I was schizophrenic. At one point they wanted to institutionalize me. But that is a story for another time. I'm less clairvoyant today."

I kept catching myself looking at Abigale's breasts, so my mind had even more difficulty trying to understand what she was saying. "I take it," I said, "you believe in reincarnation?"

She laughed. "You think? I not only believe in it, I've been with highly evolved spiritualists who have hypnotized me and taken me back to several different incarnations. The reason I am back here this time, and not with Jo-el on the other side, is because I fell in love with an unbeliever like you and had to learn not to succumb to my passions. And you know what? I am repeating that same lesson here tonight." She then placed her hands on the sides of my head with a day's worth of beard and kissed me passionately on the lips, pushing her tongue to open my lips and curling her tongue around my tongue.

"Enough spiritual talk," she said, as she came up for breath. "Where is your bedroom...."

The next morning, as Abigale and I sat on my patio, I heard my neighbor fussing around outside her house. I called over, "Trudy! Trudy! Please come over. I want to introduce you to someone."

A minute or so later, Trudy opened the door to my patio and stood there for just a moment, looking at me and Abigale. I introduced the two of them, and Trudy took a seat at the table, coffee in hand. I noticed Charles, Trudy's cat, walking in just behind her. Charles edged over toward Abigale, stopped, looked at her, and then with a howl raced out of the yard, leaving the three of us with our mouths open and amazement on our faces. Nobody said a word for a moment, and then "What was that all about?" I said. Trudy said, "Ignore her," Trudy piped up. "She acts very strange sometimes."

We picked up on the conversation as if the strange actions of Charles had never happened. Trudy began by asking Abigale questions that sounded more like an interrogation. "Where did you grow up? What were your parents like? Do you have any siblings? When did you realize that you had certain powers—predicting the future and talking with the spirits of those who had passed on?" She was particularly probing about the origin of these "special skills." Abigale answered these questions with short comments that provided little new information. She clearly was getting irritated.

She finally stood up and said she needed to get to work as she had a busy day ahead. With that, she went into the house. I could hear the shower running and some movement upstairs as she packed. She came to the back door, blew me a kiss, said she would be in touch, and then left.

Trudy looked at me and said, "She is something. I hope you know that you have gotten involved with a real tiger and an unpredictable one. If I were you, I would seriously think about breaking off any further contact with Abigale. I believe she is nothing but trouble." I was not surprised by Trudy's comments. She had always been quite frank in expressing her opinion, and I could see that she and Abigale were not soul buddies. Deep down I knew she was right. But I was still fascinated by the "tigress" and was determined to see her again.

CHAPTER THIRTY-ONE

FATHER MICHAEL

I did not know if I was falling in love with Abigale or just enjoying having passionate sex with a whirling dervish. She left a note on the bed that simply said, "Love you, Abigale."

Whenever I am troubled and can't get my mind around something, I find that if I go for a short walk in the morning, the peripatetic mind/body effort tends to allow me to begin to put things in perspective if not totally understand them. I'm an organized guy. First things first, second things second, and so on.

In walking, I reminded myself that I became acquainted with Abigale because of my Aunt Elsie's unusual accident. Secondly, I found that Elsie was concerned whether the spiritual camp run by Abigale was perhaps not on the up and up. Then I discovered Alan Brooks, also a former detective, had investigated the camp, had an unusual accident similar to Elsie's, and died shortly thereafter peculiarly. Should I be looking forward to falling down a staircase? And the séance—an experience beyond my comprehension. Who could explain that to me? Dah. A short, white-haired, bow-legged man of about eighty who took a walk each morning from St. Mary's at 8 a.m.

The next morning at 7:45 a.m., I waited for Father Michael Yeats outside of St. Mary's holding a size-medium New York Yankees sweatshirt. Right on time, Father Michael appeared, leaving the front door of the church. Spying me, he said, "The cop. You're still alive." He then began walking at his normal fast pace. I caught up to him and presented him with my gift. He stopped walking to admire it. "I never could afford one of these. I'm grateful." Then he continued walking.

Again catching up to him, I asked, "Father Michael, have you ever attended a séance?" Still walking, this five-foot two-inch priest looked up at my six-foot-three frame and said with some concern, "No, but I have counseled some of my parishioners who have."

"And what was your counsel?" I asked.

He didn't answer the question; he merely said, "Wait until we get to the bench near the beach," and then took off even faster.

When we got to the bench and sat down, he took off his New York Yankees cap and put the New York Yankees sweatshirt over his sweater. "I'm a real fan," he said. "Only attended a few games at their stadium. But used to listen to games on the radio all the time. But not anymore. Different players all the time. Not like the old days when players and teams were loyal. You like baseball?"

I moved a little closer to him. I did not mention that I bought the sweatshirt at the local Goodwill. No Vero Beach,

Florida, sports shops carried sweatshirts. "Baseball, no," I said. "Too slow a sport for me. Football. I'm a football fan. I was a Denver Broncos fan when I lived and worked in Denver. But no team in particular now since I moved to Florida. I can't get my head around the Sunshine State playing football in the fall. I miss the snow and gale winds. But Father, can you discuss what a séance is? I attended one recently at the spiritual camp outside of Vero Beach."

"Let me answer that in a roundabout way," he said, stroking the sweatshirt. "I have always been interested in God. Don't know why. My family was not particularly spiritual. At age fourteen, I signed up with a rather well-known spiritualist group. I paid my fifteen dollars. I did this by mail. The spiritualist group shipped me a package and asked me to perform the following ritual: take two candles, light them, say out loud the incantation they provided me, stand before a mirror with the candles positioned to the left and right of me, and then write back what occurred. Dutifully, I did that. After about twenty minutes or so, the mirror became cloudy and twelve faces looked out at me, one after another. All of them looked like me but were somewhat gruesome."

Father Michael, still stroking the sweatshirt, looked up at me to see if I was interested in what he was saying. I nodded at him to keep talking.

"Keep in mind, detective, I was only fourteen. I wrote back to the spiritualist group about what I experienced. Within a week or so, they got back to me by mail and told me I was now a third-degree member of their order. They also informed me that each of the faces that appeared to me were my earlier incarnations."

Father Michael stopped talking for a few moments and then grabbed my knee, which startled me a bit. He laughed and took his hand off my knee.

"I was an altar boy at the time, and when I told the priest my experience with this spiritualist group, the priest grabbed my knee just like that. I jumped a bit just like you did. But then I realized he was attempting to show his concern for me. He told me that Satan and his angelic followers are quick to respond to those of us who inhabit the Earth. God put us here on Earth to test the worthiness of our hearts and determine how obedient we are, he said. Unlike the forces of evil, God can take a long time to respond to us sometimes, especially to those God wishes to entrust with his divine works. Remember, the priest said, after Moses—who was about forty—attempted to save the enslaved Hebrews in Egypt by killing an Egyptian who was beating a Hebrew, God waited until Moses was eighty before he actually spoke to Moses. God was watching. Seeing what choices Moses made."

Father Michael touched my knee again and smiled. A kind, loving smile. "Séances demonstrate the supernatural power of supernatural beings," he said. "Somehow those supernatural powers can read our thoughts, especially about events that have traumatized us. But those supernatural beings are not of God and ultimately end up doing damage to us here on Earth if we let them."

Disturbed, I interrupted the priest and asked, "Can they possess us?"

Father Michael smiled, but it was a sad smile. "No, unless we ask them to possess us. They can do damage because they can influence us. Mess with our minds. But possession—no. God gives us free will to choose to be with the dark forces or not. But sadly, most people, like you, do not even believe such things exist."

I then told Father Michael about Abigale and all the weird circumstances that had surrounded her life. "Son, you have that crucifix I gave you?" I nodded affirmatively. "Keep it with you at all times. I'm not here to judge the woman. But she does seem troubled—and trouble especially for you because you are attracted to her." Abruptly he got up and started walking. As I caught up with him, he said, "Enough of this. Even talking about the séance troubles my very soul. Take care, my son, and thanks for the Yankee sweatshirt."

To: Verorobert@aol.com
From: Spiritabigale@aol.com

Robert:

I am so upset. I have had such great hopes for our friendship. You are the first man that I have really felt comfortable with, a man who understands me and does not just want something from me.

I will not—cannot—let go of what we have and go back to my old life. You have become too important, too critical to my well-being.

Give our friendship, our love, another chance. I refuse to let anything interfere with us.

```
    I am coming to Vero Beach next week and
would like to visit you at your aunt's house. I
will call with specific timing. We need a face-
to-face meeting, some hugs and kisses.

All my Love, Abigale
```

I decided that the note did not need an answer.

CHAPTER THIRTY-TWO

SMOTHERED

Although I had a somewhat sinking feeling that we had reached a crossroads in our relationship, I was still excited about seeing Abigale. Somehow meeting at my aunt's house was a bit disturbing. I did not know why, but I would rather have met Abigale at a restaurant.

The week went by rather slowly, but my thoughts hardly ever did not involve Abigale and our upcoming meeting at the house.

I remained concerned about her "spirits" and her connections to the "spirit" world. It was all so foreign to me—unbelievable and a bit weird. I had trouble believing in God and was skeptical about Jesus as the son of God and therefore Christianity. With this background, how could I accept the idea of spirits guiding someone's actions and their life? I was not at all sure that I could tolerate her rather unusual gifts.

I also was feeling a bit smothered by Abigale. She seemed to want control of what I did and whom I met. During the week, her emails had become quite personal, expressing strong feelings and emotions. It reminded me a bit of a girlfriend I had in college. She became very possessive and wanted me to spend every moment with her. She became jealous when I talked to other girls. Getting away from her was one of the reasons I left college and joined the military. Pretty drastic, but I could not seem to distance myself any other way. I had not reached that point with Abigale, but I had somewhat the same concerns. I could not decide what to do, how to alter my ties to Abigale without hurting her feelings or whether I should break off relations with her entirely. I felt a bit like the dog that chased the car, caught it, but then did not know what to do with it.

I decided to put my feelings on hold and wait and see how the visit with Abigale went. Maybe a face-to-face meeting would straighten things out. I really did not believe it would but tried to convince myself. She would be down to Vero in a week, and despite my concerns I was looking forward to seeing her.

CHAPTER THIRTY-THREE

THE INTERVENTION

I was sitting at home looking back over some of my aunt's notes on her computer. It was a quiet evening, and I had some classic music on the radio, pleasant and relaxing.

I heard loud knocking on the front door. Why knock loudly when you can ring the doorbell? That always disturbed me a bit because it usually meant trouble or authorities, not friends or neighbors.

Reluctantly I got to my feet and with some exasperation made my way to the front door. Opening it slowly, I expected the worst, perhaps a police officer or some other person of authority. But standing there was a middle-aged man who seemed a bit apprehensive and even puzzled. It took me a moment before I recognized him—Abigale's brother, David.

He stood there without saying a word. I invited him in. Finally, he said, "I am sorry to bother you, but I needed to talk to you about Abigale. I am with my family here in Vero and decided to look you up. I am very concerned about her well-being. You no doubt know she communicates with the 'spirits' and seems to take instructions from them and possibly give instructions to them. I find this very disturbing and believe that it is evil or at least could lead to evil's ends. I fear that the Devil is involved."

I sat down on the couch and motioned that he should sit down as well. He sat, but only on the edge of the couch. "What did you want to tell me about Abigale?"

Shaking his head as if he were trying to collect his thoughts, he then said, "I am happy that you and Abigale are getting along. You are one of the few ordinary people she seems to be attracted to." Seeming to realize he may have insult me, he quickly said, "I mean normal. I know the two of you have gotten to know each other rather well, and I came here to ask for your assistance in getting a group of friends and relatives together with her to discuss her involvement with the spirit world. Our mother's sister Aunt Hazel is interested in trying to be of help. I have done some research on what are known as 'interventions.' Most of these involved family and friends of someone who is having serious problems—drinking, drugs, and psychological issues—trying to help them resume a normal life. Sometimes the intervention is led by a trained psychologist, but often it's led by a family member who has reached the point where concern and frustration forces them to take action."

Because I had similar concerns about Abigale's involvement with "spirits," I took David's proposal seriously. But it would need to be carefully arranged, and the people involved needed to be genuinely interested in Abigale's well-being. The first and perhaps more serious problem would be to get Abigale to agree to participate in this rather personally intrusive exercise. But equally important would be to get the other participants to withhold their judgmental comments and try to address issues objectively but firmly.

I told David that I was interested in his proposal and would help in any way possible. He immediately said, "Your task is to convince Abigale to participate. I will arrange the rest, including the time, place, and other participants. I might need help in deciding who the clergyman should be."

"If you can't find one, I know just the guy," I said. David leaped to his feet, stuck out his hand, and shook mine, thanking me, then began to head to the door. It dawned on me that Abigale was not the only one in her family that was a bit unusual.

With his hand on the doorknob, he spoke about growing up with Abigale. "It was very difficult to be around her. She anticipated conversations and always seemed several steps ahead. Even as a small girl, she was always talking about what was going to happen. There seemed to be few surprises in life for her, and none for me. I found it worrisome to be in her company, and others did as well. My parents treated her with kid gloves, always giving in to her every wish and acting as if correcting her was risking something. The entire family walked around her very carefully."

After David left, I spent several hours thinking about his plan and trying to figure out how I would approach Abigale. I decided an email would be the best way of suggesting the idea. A conversation on the phone might just lead to a quick and angry rejection. I sent the following to Abigale:

From: Verorobert@aol.com
To: Spiritabigale@aol.com

Dearest Abigale:

Your brother came to see me while he was vacationing in Vero. He asked me to talk with you about sitting down with some family members and me to discuss your communication with the spirits. The objective would be for us to get a better understanding of your unique powers and for you to see how complicated it is for others to understand and accept. Your brother is concerned that there is some evil force behind this process that you do not recognize. I am less concerned about that than I am about your well-being. Because I am really fond of you, I want to do everything possible to understand your powers and the implication of exercising them.

Your friend and lover, Robert

I had no idea of the reception my email might receive. I expected the worst and waited with the proverbial bated breath. Was this the end of our relationship? Would I ever hear from her again? I was very fond of Abigale, but it was important to clear the air regarding her communications with what I considered the "dark side."

Several hours later, the telephone rang, and it was Abigale. I was surprised to hear a calm voice say, "I got the email and decided to call rather than send a note. I understand my brother's concern and yours. I do not have a problem sitting down with family members and you and discussing my relationship with the spirit world. I have been involved in several sessions such as the one David suggests and think they help clear the air. I am a bit concerned about inviting a clergyman, someone outside the family."

I said, "I think you would like this particular person. He is a retired priest, a free thinker and a calm presence." She responded, "Okay. I will withhold judgment until I meet him. I am ready to be grilled any afternoon next week." I suggested Wednesday afternoon, with a dinner involving all of us in the evening.

That had been much easier than I expected. I breathed a sigh of relief and called David to report on the success of my mission. David was very excited and said he had found a room where the group could meet and was pleased to be given a precise time and date.

Wednesday came more quickly than I was prepared for. Five of us—Abigale, David, Aunt Hazel, Father Michael, and I—gathered in front of a small building on 14th Street in Vero. The rooms in the building were regularly rented to various social groups and associations for their meetings. David had asked for a small room with a round table that would easily seat the five of us. Someone met us at the door and showed us where we were to meet. The room was plainly decorated and quite pleasant. The table was at least ten feet across and made of some beautiful, exotic wood. On top of the table was a large pitcher of ice water and several glasses. Arrayed around the table were five very comfortable leather-upholstered chairs. It was just right for the meeting we were about to hold.

It was an interesting and rather odd group of people that sat around the table. Clearly the most striking person present was Abigale with her bright red hair, striking figure, and beautiful face. She seemed very calm and controlled. David, looking very much like a real estate salesman with carefully cut hair and deep tan, sat nervously tapping his fingers on the table. He had a pad with notes on it in front of him, and he was clearly a bundle of nerves. His right leg kept moving up and down, which he seemingly did not have any control over. Aunt Hazel was the picture of everyone's aunt with gray hair cut short and a round and appealing face that often was smiling. She possessed a wonderful laugh that came out sometimes when nothing being said was funny. I assumed the laugh was her default mechanism when she became uncomfortable. I had picked up Father Michael at the church. He looked a young eighty years, but the slight stoop and very white hair gave away his age. He was wearing the same sweater he wore when I first encountered him a few months earlier, although the temperature outside was touching eighty degrees.

After introductions and some polite exchanges, David started off the meeting saying that he had called everyone together to exchange views and discuss some issues that he believed should be of concern to all present—a somewhat murky introduction. David said he had asked Father Michael to be the discussion leader because he had no direct connection with any of the participants and would be a neutral third party.

Father Michael said he would do the best he could to have a—and here he paused seeming to search for a word—"fruitful" session. He said he had been involved in several so-called interventions and believed they tended to have positive outcomes. I looked at Abigale to see if there was any response to Father Michael using the word "intervention." She showed no outward reaction at all. Cool and collected, although she did uncross her legs and recross them in the opposite direction. Father Michael then stressed the importance of polite and calm discussion; he asked all of us to listen and said that he would try to find time for everyone to comment on what they heard. If someone wanted to make a comment, they should signal to him, and he would find an appropriate time. I decided my best course of action was to say nothing at all.

"In conversations with David and Robert," Father Michael said, looking directly at Abigale, "I think we should begin with the following outline of topics to discuss. First, the observation from David that Abigale even as a child seemed capable of predicting the future. Second, that Abigale now serves as the intermediary between those who have passed on and people trying to get in touch with them. Finally, Abigale seems to be in direct communication with spirits that suggest to her what to do and what to avoid." Father Michael then nodded his head toward Abigale to address the first issue: predicting the future.

Abigale had no hesitation explaining her ability to see into the future. It was the result of instincts and skills she developed at a very young age: Observation. Watching what was going on. Listening. Paying careful attention to what people were saying. Using common sense to anticipate the outcome of events. There was no magic in all of this. Sometimes luck was involved, but more often it was just logic. There were a few comments and examples presented by the group demonstrating Abigale's skill at predicting events. There was general acceptance that what she described made sense and was more a heightened awareness than anything spiritual.

The next topic would prove to be a bit more contentious—acting as an intermediary between the spirit world and the real world. Abigale was asked by Father Michael to address this issue. Abigale, seemingly dismissing Father Michael altogether, looked directly at me and said, "It is really not that complicated. People, often in great distress, ask me to get in touch with a loved one or a person of particular interest who had passed on. Sometimes I am able to establish contact. Many times, it takes three or four sessions before I can make contact with their loved one. But, it has little to do with me. I am merely the communications channel. I am the conduit for information. Often, I have no clear idea or memory of the information that I convey. I also have no idea whether it is accurate—fact or fiction. The spirits are well intentioned. I know that. I stake my life on that. But sometimes, I have found they provide misinformation for some greater purpose or good to help whomever they are reaching out to. Perhaps they don't want to sadden the inquirer more than they have to. Sometimes those who have passed on are not very good people. Perhaps even terrible people. Sometimes the people who have passed are evil and may even wish to harm the inquirer."

There was considerable discussion from the other participants about how she got in contact with people who had passed on. Abigale said she did not know how or why people on the "other side" chose to use her as an intermediary. She said she thought that there were spirits that seek out ways of communicating with those left behind and that she was just chosen as a vehicle. "From as young as I can remember," she said, looking directly at her nephew David, "I always wanted to be helpful to others. Especially those who were suffering like I suffered when my dad and mother died in a terrible fire when they were asleep. I think that's when the spirits first let me know that they were willing to use me to communicate with those who had passed."

Father Michael then interrupted Abigale to broach the final topic involving "spirits" communicating with Abigale and offering advice and warnings on relationships and life choices. She could not clearly describe how that information was transmitted, it just appeared in her mind and became part of her thoughts, decisions, and actions. She mentioned that she had received warnings that her parents were considering calling on an exorcist and that her boyfriend and her minister friend were acting in ways not in her best interest. She also said, again looking directly at me, that the spirits informed her that my aunt and her detective as well as others were writing things that would harm the camp. Then Abigale mentioned that the spirits had warned her to be careful in her relationship with Robert and were particularly concerned about Father Michael and his God. The group let out a collective gasp. When she mentioned Father Michael's name, she looked directly at him, swished her beautiful red hair across her face and back again, and smiled at him. Perhaps it was more of a smirk than a smile. Father Michael did not react at all.

I had some of the same skills as Abigale when it came to learning from watching others and getting silent signals. It was clear to me that Father Michael was holding back on his judgments about what Abigale was saying about her connections to the spirit world. He was playing the role of moderator. But it was also clear that he had serious reservations about what Abigale seemed to be describing as normal behavior. If the objective of the intervention was to get Abigale to recognize that she needed to free herself from the spirits, it was a failure. It appeared to me and to others at the meeting that Abigale saw nothing wrong with turning a blind eye even to evil acts if they benefited her.

There was no neat ending to the discussion. It just trailed off as the group ran out of steam. In any case, it was apparent to all that the meeting was over, and we all left for a break before dinner at the Ocean Grill.

I took the opportunity of the time before dinner to talk with both David and Aunt Hazel. I wanted to get their private views on Abigale. David had far more to say than Hazel, and he was very critical of his sister. As he said in one of our earlier conversations, his relations with Abigale were strained at best. He tried to avoid her, staying out of her way as much as possible, but in a small family that was difficult. He said, "I never introduced her to my friends because she could be very nasty. Also, she seemed to delight in embarrassing me, pointing out my flaws and limitations." Perhaps the most damning comments were those describing Abigale maneuvering to get others in trouble. Small lies about their behavior, focusing on the negative aspects of things they had done. He summed it up, saying, "She is not a nice person; she is a troublemaker and seemed to delight in that role. She is vindictive and holds grudges."

As we were parting, David gave me an envelope. He said, "This contains two letters about Abigale. I have never shared them with anyone before. I probably should have given them to you before the intervention, but I did not want to prejudice your thinking."

Aunt Hazel had a rather different take on Abigale. She thought her niece was very smart and ambitious. "I always thought she would become a famous person, either in a university setting or some other successful undertaking. She has a particular talent for anticipating what was going to happen, how some particular problem would be resolved, and who would benefit from it. She can read people very well and instinctively knows how they will react in various situations. That can make some people uncomfortable."

It was a mixed picture presented by the two of them.

The conversation at dinner tended to avoid subjects discussed earlier and was surprisingly anodyne. It was interesting to observe the group in a more relaxed atmosphere. Everyone ordered drinks, but the type of drinks they asked for revealed something about them. Abigale had a white wine, David a beer, Aunt Hazel a tropical fancy drink topped by a small red umbrella, Father Michael Irish whiskey, and I had a gin martini. Dinner orders were similarly different. Abigale had a large Caesar salad with anchovies on the side, David scallops, Aunt Hazel shrimp, Father Michael pompano, and I had a medium rare porterhouse steak. The drinks and meals seemed to match the personalities.

David and Aunt Hazel were staying overnight in a nearby hotel. Abigale and I drove Father Michael home in my car. He had consumed a few shots of Irish whiskey and was slightly inebriated. During the drive back to Father Michael's small home near St. Mary's, where he lived with other priests, everyone in the car was silent. But once we had arrived and I was about to get out of my car to assist Father Michael from the car, he asked if he could speak to Abigale. With some feeling of trepidation, I stayed put and looked at him as he addressed Abigale. She remained in the front seat and did not turn around to look at the diminutive priest.

In a voice much stronger and sterner than I thought he was capable of, Father Michael said, "I did not speak up during the session this afternoon because I was concerned about the feelings of your brother and aunt, and I was playing the role of moderator. I want to say now as clearly as possible that I believe you are the handmaid of the Devil. Not just a tool, because tools have no guilt in the actions they perform. You, on the other hand, know precisely what you are doing. Your role is not that of an innocent but is directly connected to the evil act. Ordinarily I would pray for you and ask forgiveness, but I believe you are fully in the company of the Devil and beyond redemption." I looked at Abigale for any reaction. Her eyes fluttered a bit but the expression on her face actually looked somewhat serene.

As I helped Father Michael out of the car, he turned and addressed Abigale one more time. This time his voice was filled with compassion. "Do not harm Robert."

Abigale turned to looked at Father Michael. Clearly now there was a combination of disdain and rage on her face. Under her breathe I heard her say, "Go talk to your God, you foolish old man." He heard the comment. But merely shrugged his shoulders and gave me a very sad look.

We drove to my house without saying a word to each other. Once inside Abigale asked if the guest bedroom was made up. It was pretty clear she was not spending the night in my bed. She went into the bedroom and quietly but firmly shut the door. A bit later, I heard the shower and then silence.

I poured myself a brandy and sat in the living room for a considerable time, pondering the events of the day and evening. My relationship with Abigale was over, and I felt relieved. It had been a difficult affair. One thing was clear: Abigale could not look at herself or her behavior with anything resembling objectivity. As I was hanging up my jacket, I saw the envelope I had placed in the jacket's inside pocket that David had given me earlier in the evening. Opening it, I found two letters, both addressed to David's parents. I don't know how David had gotten these letters. They could have been given to him by his parents, or he might have found them at their house.

The first letter was handwritten. It started with an apology to Abigale's parents saying that the writer was uncertain whether it was a good idea to have written. But it was something she felt she needed to do. She said she had been a close friend of Abigale's during their sophomore and junior years in high school. They took some of the same courses and were involved in a few activities together. They were good friends. Then, in their senior year, the relationship fell apart. The reason was that over time she had discovered Abigale had some serious faults. She consistently demonstrated cruel and demeaning behavior toward others. She sought recognition for everything she did and believed she was entitled to more than others. She was willing to manipulate the facts or the situation for her own gain. She wrote the letter because she was convinced many, including her parents, had an idealized view of Abigale that would allow her to do real harm.

The second letter was from a therapist that Abigale had been seeing at her parent's insistence. The therapist had summarized her thoughts after four sessions.

> *Dear Mr. and Mrs. Cruz,*
>
> *At your request, I had four sessions with your daughter Abigale. I will provide a detailed report, but what follows is a summary of my conclusions about your daughter.*
>
> *Abigale initially was very reticent about sharing her feelings and expressing her views and concerns. But after a couple of sessions, she began to speak more frankly and became quite open about her attitudes and behavior. Abigale is a very bright and articulate teenager, considerably more grown up than most girls her age. She is quite outspoken and has well developed*

> *views on most subjects. She has a great memory and vocabulary and is well schooled in the basic subjects of history, math, and science.*
>
> *Abigale does have some serious problems in her relationships with others. Perhaps most concerning is what appears to be a total lack of empathy. She does not express any understanding of the feelings of others and is excessively concerned about her own feelings and attitudes. When asked about her relationships with other students or adults, she is inclined to refer back to her goals and achievements.*
>
> *Abigale will not directly admit it, but she clearly is very manipulative and calculating when it comes to personal relations. The question that always seems to be in the back of her mind is "what is in it for me?"*
>
> *Abigale has a great capacity for covering up her willingness to achieve her goals at the expense of others. She is very calculating and devious but knows how to present a "good" face.*
>
> *I would take Abigale's flaws very seriously. She has the capacity to be manipulative and misleading. This characteristic is so strong and so unlikely to change that she could be dangerous to herself and others.*

My immediate reaction was that both of these assessments were far too harsh. But I recognized the truth in some of the statements. After all, I had come to the conclusion that some of Abigale's actions were evil. On the spur of the moment, I decided to take a look at the internet to see what was considered evil and why. Quite by accident, the first article that came up was one titled "Dark personality theory: the nine traits of evil people in your life." The article was based on studies by a research team from Germany and Denmark. The studies aimed to determine whether there was a scientific way of "defining the extent to which someone is evil." In conclusion, a set of nine statements were developed and the person being tested was asked if they strongly agreed or disagreed with each. If you were strongly in agreement with all nine, there was a high likelihood that you would rank high on the "evil" scale. The statements were:

It is hard to get ahead without cutting corners here and there.
I like to use clever manipulation to get my way.
People who get mistreated have usually done something to bring it upon themselves.
I know I am special because everyone keeps telling me so.
I honestly feel I'm just more deserving than others.
I'll say anything to get what I want.
Hurting people would be exciting.
I try to make sure others know about my successes.
It is sometimes worth a little suffering on my part to see others receive the punishment they deserve.

A thought crossed my mind. I could knock on the door of the guest room, wake up Abigale, and ask her to take the test. I wondered what the result would be. Not a good idea. Instead, I decided it was time for me to go to bed by myself.

The next morning, we had breakfast together with polite but cold conversation. Clearly there was going to be no making up; the break was neat and clean. I thought of my conversation with my ex-wife, Susan. Maybe I was too quick to brush her off and continue my relationship with Abigale. Susan seemed like a safe haven in comparison to Abigale. Maybe I would give her a call and ask her to come down to Vero. We could see if the relationship could be rekindled or if it was too late. Or maybe I should just go back to my old life which, in thinking about it now, was not all that bad. At least it was peaceful and far less stressful.

I drove Abigale to pick up her car, which she had parked where we had gathered yesterday, and we drove separately to my aunt's house. I got there first and met her at the door.

CHAPTER THIRTY-FOUR

DON'T BET AGAINST THE HOUSE

"I could feel the aura of the house just walking up to it," Abigale said. "The spirits are here in force." That worried me a bit. All I needed was a house full of spirits greeting Abigale and trying to push me out.

We began talking about the history of the house. It turned out she knew more about its history than I did. She asked what I intended to do with the house. When I said that I had not decided whether to keep it or sell it, she became very insistent that I sell the house to the camp. She argued that the house had a long connection with the camp, suggesting that if I did not sell to them, she was afraid something would happen to me. Again, those threatening spirits lingered in the background of her warnings.

I was about to turn the conversation to the end of our relationship and mention that I felt uncomfortable with the idea of "spirits" guiding her actions. I wanted to ask exactly what kind of control they exerted over her and how she planned to deal with them in the future. Then I decided that this line of discussion would lead nowhere.

We had little to say to one another. Silence was not a bad alternative. But just then my cell phone rang. I answered it only to hear a loud voice yelling, "What did you do to Father Michael last night?" It took me a second to identify the caller as the woman at the church who had put me in contact with Father Michael.

I responded, "What are you talking about? Has something happened to him?"

The caller said, "I am sorry; I should have started with some information before accusing you of being responsible. Last night Father Michael died of a massive heart attack."

I was speechless, and it took me a while to get my bearings. After expressing my sorrow about his death and offering to be of any help, I sadly disconnected from the distraught woman, turned to Abigale, and said, "Father Michael died of a heart attack last night." To my horror, a slight smile flashed over Abigale's face. I stared at her, dumbstruck. She was an evil person!

A noise from upstairs interrupted our thoughts. We both heard it. It sounded like a door scraping along the floor. My immediate assumption was that someone had opened the "door to nowhere." I told Abigale to stay where she was, and I got to my feet to investigate what was going on upstairs.

I made my way up the stairs. I remembered suddenly that I had forgotten to put on the wooden crucifix given to me by Father Michael. It lay on my desk at townhouse on Cardinal. I had been wearing it on a regular basis.

The door to the bedroom was open. I walked in and saw that the door at the end of the room was open as well. Perhaps the wind had blown it open. Walking over, I looked down into the yard. I heard what sounded like footsteps behind me, and I smelled ginger. I started to turn, but before I could move, I felt the pressure of hands on my shoulders pushing me out the door. I was falling—headfirst!

What follows is Abigale's statement to the police when they asked her about Robert's death.

"When we heard a noise upstairs, Robert started up the stairs. My first reaction was to follow him. I did, and on the way, I grabbed my phone out of my purse, thinking that I should make a record of what we might find upstairs. I put the phone on video and quickly ran up the stairs. I reached the door to the bedroom and stopped. Robert was standing in the open door at the other end of the room, looking down. He seemed to turn just a bit but then raised his arms and hurtled out the open door as if he had been pushed.

"I rushed over to the open door and looked down at Robert's body on the patio. I filmed all of this and kept the video on as I ran down the stairs into the backyard. Rushing over to Robert, I felt his neck and wrist for a pulse. I found none. I believe I said to Robert, 'I loved you and am so sorry that you got involved with me. This should never have happened.'"

Abigale's statement was confirmed by the police upon reviewing the video and voice recording. The police did ask what she discussed with Mr. McKenzie before he went upstairs. She answered that she was truly sorry that she had got involved with him and that he had invited her to his diseased aunt's house. They also asked why after she entered the room the video did not show her walking toward Robert and instead recorded erratic pictures of the floor and room. Abigale said she was so worried about Robert that she was not paying any attention to the camera.

* * *

The death was ruled "accidental" in unusual circumstances.

About a year later, Elsie's—or more precisely, Robert's—house was put up for sale. Within days, someone from the camp bought the house without an inspection or even a walk-through. They knew its history.

CHAPTER THIRTY-FIVE

THE SURVEILLANCE

Sitting outdoors on her patio, Trudy heard voices from next door—Robert's townhouse. She was not surprised, as real estate salespeople had been showing the house over the past week. This all brought back the sad memories of Robert's death. With those memories came a rush of feelings about Robert's evil love—what was her name—Abigale. She was a real witch.

Trudy wondered what had happened to the house where both Robert and his aunt died. She knew it had been put up for sale by Robert's estate, but she did not know who bought it. Something to look into—and she made a note to herself to do just that. It would be easy to find what houses had been sold recently, and she had the address of Robert's house.

The next day she asked one of her real estate friends to look into who bought Robert's house. She was not greatly surprised to find that the Spiritual and Health Camp was the buyer. Robert had mentioned how much Abigale wanted to buy the house.

All this led to a new idea: Trudy would ask Sheila Turney, who she had met at the various events held after Robert's death, about joining her to spy on his old house and see what was going on there. She called Sheila, saying, "You may remember me—Trudy. We met at some of the events after Robert's death."

After a short pause, Sheila said, "Certainly I remember you. What can I do for you?"

Trudy said, "I have a rather bizarre proposal, although it makes sense to me at this moment. I would like you to join me in surveillance of Robert's house in Osceola Park. I am not sure what it will accomplish, but I just want to see what is going on there, who is living there or visiting. Obviously, I am most interested to see if Abigale has moved in. Abigale had Robert totally hoodwinked and under her spell. I would not be surprised if she killed him."

There was a moment of silence, and Trudy did not know if Sheila had hung up or was still there. Then Sheila, with somewhat of a chuckle, said, "That is a strange idea, but something that I would like to do." Trudy told Sheila that early Saturday morning she would pick her up at her condo, and they would reconnoiter Robert's house in Osceola. Sheila agreed, and that was the beginning of an unusual mission.

The next Saturday, she picked Sheila up at her condo. She was dressed in dark clothes and wore a black baseball cap, ready for spying. They drove across the bridge into old Vero and after some hits and misses found Robert's house. They parked down the street a bit, on the same side of the street as the house, and sat there watching the front door. Nothing happened; there was absolutely no activity on the street, let alone at the house. They had a thermos of coffee and some donuts. Trudy said, "This is silly; what are we waiting for, and what do we expect to see?"

Sheila was much more patient and said, "I have read a lot of detective stories and long periods of waiting are routine during surveillance operations. We should just sit here and wait."

Both of the women dozed for a while, and then they saw the front door open to Elsie's former house with an outside door to nowhere. Out came Abigale. She was staying at the house. She got into a car and drove to a store on Old Dixie Road where she bought some pastries. They followed her back to the house and sat there a few minutes before deciding that their best course of action was to go to the First Watch restaurant for breakfast. Abigale was not likely to go anywhere soon, and besides, they had accomplished our task—discovering that Abigale was spending weekends at the house she had "stolen" from Robert.

Over the next month, Trudy and Sheila regularly got together and drove over to the house in Osceola, parking in the same place and watching the front door. Sometimes they followed Abigale on her trips to the grocery store or drug store. As far as they could determine, she did not vary her destinations very much. They established her routine for visiting Vero. She came down on Friday afternoon and left on Sunday morning or late on Saturday. Once in a while, she would stay at the house during the week. What was the purpose of this surveillance? Probably neither Trudy nor Sheila could explain why they were doing this other than supporting the memory of Robert. Trudy did give Sheila considerable background on Abigale's history based on what Robert had told her. She mentioned the trail of death that seem to follow Abigale. She also emphasized what Robert had said about what seemed to be a total lack of sympathy or empathy or the misfortunes of others. Sheila's response was one of astonishment. She asked, "What can be done to stop that woman?"

* * *

They changed their surveillance routine a bit and decided to stake out Abigale's house in the late afternoon on a Sunday. It was warm, and Trudy decided to park under a large oak tree somewhat farther down the street than usual. There was a soft wind blowing, and they had the car windows down. It was very pleasant, and they talked about how enjoyable it was for the pair to conduct surveillance. Sheila said, "Maybe we could hire ourselves out to some detective agency and make a little money." Their laughter was cut short as the door to Abigale's house opened, and she stepped out, dressed to the nines, and walked to her car.

They followed her through town, over the bridge to the Costa d'Este Beach Resort. Abigale parked in the lot and went into the hotel. Trudy stopped in front of the hotel, and Sheila went up to the glass doors to see if she could determine what Abigale was doing. Sheila felt safe getting that close because she had never met Abigale. She saw Abigale at the bar ordering a drink and then decided to return to the car. It did not make sense for them to wait around.

They continued their surveillance routine. One Saturday morning as they were parked in the usual place Sheila asked Trudy why she named her female cat Charles. "When I bought her, I thought she was a male because she was so big." Trudy laughed. "I so wanted a man in my life, I guess. I never looked to see that she was a she. It's probably why I've had few men in my life."

Suddenly there was a knock on the window of the car. A bit startled, they both turned, and there stood Abigale with a scowl on her face. Rolling down the window, Sheila said, "Hello, what can I do for you?"

Abigale said in a voice filled with anger, "You can stop spying on me. If you do not, I will call the police and have you arrested. Now get out of here and leave me alone."

Trudy was not intimidated and said, "We know you seduced Robert and then murdered him. I hope your actions do not rest easily on your conscience." Trudy then started the car and quickly accelerated, leaving Abigale standing on the curb fuming.

The incident with Abigale did not deter the intrepid spy team. They were back parked at the house the next Sunday morning—this time a bit earlier than usual. It was unusual to see a car parked in front of the house, a black sedan. They saw the door to the house open, and out came a man. Trudy thought the person looked familiar but could not see him clearly. He returned to the door for a kiss from a woman standing in the shadow of the door. He then went to the car and drove away, but not before Sheila had taken out her small binoculars, copied down his license plate number, and noted that the car was a BMW. Trudy quickly started their car and followed the black sedan. This was getting exciting.

They followed the car across the bridge and onto the island. It stopped about a block from the beach and pulled into a small parking lot. Trudy parked on the street and watched the man get out of the car and walk into a small office building that she had visited many times. She recognized him now—it was Henry Stimson, her financial advisor. She was shocked because she knew Henry rather well. He was married and had three young children—twin girls about eleven and a boy of eight or so. What was going on between Henry and Abigale? It was bad news, whatever it was.

After dropping Sheila off at her condo, Trudy went home and immediately called Henry Stimson's office. She knew his secretary and decided to collect some information. She did find out that Henry's wife and children were visiting parents in Virginia. Trudy knew that Henry regularly walked over to the Costa d'Este Beach Resort for a drink in the evening. That habit must have led to meeting Abigale. It did not take much imagination to figure out what happened then. Trudy did not have a lot of sympathy for Henry. He was a grown man who should know better. She did feel bad for Henry's wife and children and knew that Henry was just a plaything for Abigale. She did not care about his family or what would happen to the marriage. She was just exercising her power over men.

Trudy and Sheila talked and decided that they should end their spying program against Abigale. They had found out a bit about what was happening at the house. More importantly, they may have caused her some discomfort. But what were they going to do about her affair with Henry Stimson? They just could not let it go on until Henry and his family were destroyed. They would have to do something.

CHAPTER THIRTY-SIX

A TOAST TO ABIGALE

Picking up the newspaper from the front steps, Trudy noticed another couple looking at Robert's townhouse next door. Apparently, few like to buy a house if which the owner had died somewhat mysteriously. Usually, when one of these townhouses came for sale, there were often a number of people ready to lay down a good deal of money and even bid against others. Trudy was not thinking of what a good deal she had gotten when she bought her townhouse; she was thinking about how much she missed Robert. But foremost in her mind were thoughts of how much damage Abigale had done to everyone she came in contact with. She was an evil person, without a doubt.

She looked at the front page of the local paper and saw the headline that read "Local Spiritualist Apparently Dies in House Fire." There on the front page was a picture of the house she and Sheila had been watching over the past month or so. The house was totally engulfed in flames. The story reported that the fire began in the middle of the night and raged out of control until the early morning. Firemen reported seeing a figure, believed to be a woman, standing in a door on the second story of the house just before it collapsed. This door just opened out into nothing.

According to the reporter, when the house was built by a spiritualist in the 1930s, the door had been put in to allow spirits to enter and leave the house whenever they wished. At the time the story was being written, there was no information about whether or not firemen found human remains in the house or what was left of it. The story went on to describe when the house was built and that its current owner, the spiritualist camp north of Vero Beach, had informed the police that their church minister and camp director Abigale Cruz had been living in the house.

The next day, the paper continued reporting on the fire. Apparently, the remains of only one person had been uncovered, but the real news was that the fire inspector had determined that an accelerant, probably gasoline, had been spread around the foundation of the house and then ignited. That meant that a murder had been committed. Trudy read all this very carefully and then called Sheila. She asked, "Could we meet for lunch at the Ocean Grill? We probably need to talk."

Sheila answered, "I would be delighted to have lunch with you."

They walked into the grill at exactly noon and were seated at a window table. Ordinarily, neither of the two would have a drink for lunch, but this was a special occasion. Sheila ordered a gin martini, in honor of Robert, and Trudy a cosmopolitan. They sat quietly for a moment, looking at each other, both smiling, and then Sheila said, "Revenge is a drink best served cold," raising her glass to touch Trudy's.

Gasoline
Gasoline

ACKNOWLEDGMENTS

Many thanks to Anthony Ziccardi, publisher of Post Hill Press, for his encouragement for this novel.